For JoAnn —
with love
Alepis

KISS ME OVER THE GARDEN GATE

ALEXIS RANKIN POPIK

AUCOOT PRESS

Boston

AUCOOT PRESS

For Bill

In Memory of
Judith Selverstone Shaw
and
Tom Caselli

PART ONE

CHAPTER ONE

Monday, September 25, 1995

AT FIRST CLARE DIDN'T REALIZE HER HUSBAND WAS MISSING. IT WAS UNUSUAL, though, for him to be late and not call. Since she and their boys joined him in Los Angeles last month, Richard had developed the habit of calling her from his car phone on the way home for a few minutes of uninterrupted conversation. Sometimes it was their only chance to talk. Even then, she had to settle for fragments as Richard made his way home, losing him as he maneuvered below overpasses and dropped into canyons, reconnecting when he reached a clear space, sometimes cut off entirely until the moan of their automatic garage door heralded his safe return. But that night, a September Monday of hot, dry winds, a day so scorching that the quail on their hill crouched beneath the scrub until the sun finally set, he didn't call and he didn't come home.

She stood at the living room window in a space she had cleared among the stacks of unpacked boxes, absent-mindedly watching for Richard's car while a stream of commuting parents and car-pooling mothers with their vans of soccer players sped past. She didn't know these people but had learned over the past few weeks to recognize their Lexuses and Suburbans. She made up names for them: Show Biz, with his pony tail and car phone, and Skunk Woman, who had a dramatic slash of white through her unnaturally black hair. Her new neighbors couldn't see Clare watching them because her house's windows, like their own, were tinted to shield against the blistering Southern California sun.

"Where's Dad?" Adam asked, coming to stand beside her. He slipped one thin brown arm around his mother's waist. Bending down to him, she kissed the top of his silky dark hair. He wasn't wearing shoes and his tan, bare feet were flat and almost archless, small duplicates of Richard's. Richard. She probably forgot what he told her about his schedule. She forgot everything these days.

"Where is he, Mom?" Adam asked again.

Clare stroked his hair, pulling it away from his eyes.

"At a meeting."

~⌒

"Mom?" Matt called. "Can we order pizza? I'm starving."

Clare glanced at her watch. Seven thirty. No wonder Matt was hungry. How many mothers forget to feed their children? Probably more than would admit it, but still … She sat with Matt and Adam while they wolfed down the pizza; it was the least she could do. They, too, seemed untethered, so far from their much-loved hometown of Alameda on the cool shores of San Francisco Bay, so far from their friends. She had driven them around town that morning, looking for spots where ten- and fourteen-year-olds might congregate, but they had found nothing—just stretches of vacant parks and empty white sidewalks, glaring back at the sun.

"Maybe it's too hot," Adam said. "Maybe all the kids stay inside where it's cool."

"Or live somewhere else, where it's fun," Matt added, sliding his eyes sideways to see if Clare got the message.

"It'll be fun here, as soon as school starts," she promised. "You'll see.

It just takes time."

"Fun," Matt muttered, turning away.

After dinner the boys retreated to the family room to watch television and Clare took a glass of Chardonnay to the patio. The sun had dropped behind the Simi Hills and it was finally cool enough to sit outside. That's what LA was supposed to be good for—outdoor living. As she sipped her wine, Merlin, a neighbor's cat, came by, picking his way carefully along the top of the gray cement block walls that separated their subdivision's lots.

"How do you know his name is Merlin?" she asked Adam last month. "His tag says so," he pointed out, though Clare hadn't realized the cat had a tag, his coat was so thick around his neck. It stood out like a little ruff and made him look medieval.

"Does he belong to one of your friends?"

She waited for Matt to remind her that they didn't have any friends but instead Adam got in the first word, telling her that a kid three houses down said Merlin belonged to a "scary old lady with lots of cats" who lived around the corner on Ridgeway. It was hard to imagine an old woman living anywhere near here. Elderly people seemed an artifact of another time, a different place. Clare hadn't seen anyone in the entire town who appeared to be over forty.

Merlin was the first neighbor—except for Jannie—to greet her when they moved into the house in August. She had found him sitting in what became his usual place atop their back fence, staring into their yard with intense but polite interest. Over the weeks she had come to look forward to his visits and found herself checking the fence for Merlin's silhouette against the backdrop of dry hills. Merlin seemed to understand that she was uneasy among the scrub-and-yucca-covered hillsides and that his presence comforted her.

That evening, the cat accompanied Clare on her inspection of the scraggly shrubbery the previous owners had planted—juniper and fortnight lilies: low maintenance, drought-resistant and hideous. She kicked at a rock-hard

3

clod of adobe and it disintegrated, insinuating dust into the openwork of her sandal. She pulled off her shoes and lowered one foot, then the other, into their swimming pool, washing the grit off her toes. The cool water felt good. She dropped to the pool's edge, careful not to spill the wine, and dangled her legs in the water. Merlin rubbed against her back, but when she turned to pet him he retreated to a forlorn tangle of orange sun azaleas. She sighed. In her ignorance, she had imagined her new garden in Los Angeles would be a lush, tropical paradise like the grounds of celebrity mansions in *Architectural Digest*. Steven Spielberg's Malibu home, a beautiful Mediterranean, was featured on one of the magazine's covers; she kept it at her bedside in Alameda, examining in detail the tall palms and bright bougainvillea cascading over stucco walls. It was to be her consolation for moving: endless sun, a gentle climate. But instead of Malibu, they had landed in Agave: hot, dry, and desiccated by afternoon winds, their new yard crowded with a haphazard collection of sad botanical orphans slowly suffocating in the clay of their cut-and-filled hillside.

"I'll hire somebody to help you," Richard told her. "One of my clients is a great gardener. She'll know a good landscaper. Trust me."

A landscape architect had seemed an unnecessary extravagance, but in this climate and place, Clare knew she would need help.

Richard was true to his word. Last Saturday morning a landscape architect, Steve Rosado, appeared promptly at nine, his portfolio tucked under one arm. Rosado. She wondered if the word meant "rose" in Spanish. He was beautiful like a rose. They sat together in the sun on a wrought iron bench while Merlin took up residence on Clare's feet, gazing at her from the center of his chrysanthemum ruff. Clare wondered if the occasional light touch of Steve's arm against hers was intentional. It seemed so, but maybe that was her imagination, a lonely housewife's fantasy. If only Merlin would stop staring.

She pored over the portfolio, asking why he had made this or that choice in a particular garden. While they talked, Richard buzzed around like a deranged dragonfly, refilling coffee cups, appearing with plates of fruit. Occasionally he interrupted with a comment about a landscape they were discussing, though he knew nothing at all about gardens. She wanted to tell him to settle down, just sit still for a minute. She would have said that if Rosado hadn't been here. When Richard got like that—too excited, too enthusiastic—and they were with other people, she would squeeze his hand or press his arm, a signal for him to slow down a bit. But she couldn't do that this morning; he had already rushed off to the kitchen again. He was trying so hard to make her happy.

Clare smiled at Steve Rosado. "I really like your work. But I can't imagine what you'll be able to do with this mess of ours."

"I spend almost as much time thinking about the site and talking to the clients about it as I do actually landscaping," Steve said. "You may get tired of me."

She doubted she would ever get tired of him.

"Don't worry," Steve said, one hand on her shoulder. "You can have a lovely garden in Los Angeles."

That was Saturday.

~⊃

Merlin returned for a second brush against her back, then a third, purring like a toy helicopter. Clare heaved herself up, then reached into the pocket of her shorts for the kitty treats she had taken to carrying around for him. She sighed again as she bent and held out her hand to the cat. A lovely garden. She looked at the wind-shredded rose bushes and sunburnt impatience. Lovely indeed. Merlin brushed against her bare leg in farewell, then disappeared.

Clare settled into one of the patio chairs. A few minutes more and she would check on the boys. She tilted her head back and raked through the sides of her hair with her fingers. She had to do something about her hair; it was as scraggly and dry as bunch grass. She would have to find a hairdresser. And a dentist. And a doctor. And some friends, even one friend would be enough. Someone besides a cat.

The only friend she had here was Richard. Richard. She drummed her fingers on the table. Why was he so late? She took a gulp of wine. He would be home soon, she was sure. She smiled, anticipating his arrival. It was a comfort just to think about him. She looked forward to the sound of his key in the lock at night, the way he cleared his throat before he kissed her, as if he were embarrassed, and the slightly distracted manner in which he would rummage through the kitchen drawers, looking for the wine opener. He seldom found it and would turn to her for help. Clare was the finder, the person in the house who knew where everything was. But not here. She couldn't remember where anything was in this new house: not the cups nor the silverware, not even her husband.

She wandered into the family room where Matt and Adam sat, rapt, watching a news shot of a freeway—"Live from Chopper Five" ran the tag line across the bottom of the screen—and a newsman was narrating excitedly:

"Ginny, you can see this live shot of The 10 right now, just east of The 405 interchange. The suspect, driving a dark green pickup, was apparently stopped by police on The 405. When asked for identification, the suspect sped off in his vehicle, running down the officer who detained him."

A pickup truck, tailed by police cruisers with flashing lights, was racing past cars that had slowed and were moving into the far right lanes of the freeway.

"How seriously was the officer injured, Bob?"

There was a pause. "Uh, Ginny, I don't have anything definite on that yet."

Clare moved closer to the television. "What's going on?"

"It's a car chase, Mom," Matt explained. "They're on TV here all the time. The cops try to catch somebody, and the news helicopter puts it on TV. You can watch the cops chase them. Sometimes they shoot out their tires."

As if on cue, the announcer pointed out that the police were shooting at the tires, and the pickup lurched from side to side, then pulled to a halt. Police cars swarmed behind it and officers emerged, crouched low with guns drawn as they approached the truck's cab. The picture wavered as the helicopter tried for a closer shot. The pickup's driver was pulled roughly from the car and pushed to the ground, face down, arms and legs spread-eagled. He was quickly surrounded by a ring of police.

"Are they going to hurt him, Mom?" Adam asked.

"No, Honey," Clare replied, deciding as she retreated to the kitchen that it was best not to go into the encounter between Rodney King and the LAPD, the "not guilty of excessive force" verdict rendered in nearby Simi Valley, and the riots that ensued. She poured another glass of Chardonnay and took the portable phone back out to the patio where the boys couldn't hear.

First she tried Richard's office. As the phone rang, Clare imagined him, worn out from the day's work, snoozing on the capacious couch in his new office, a corner suite Wentworth and Berg had provided as part of the enticement to join the partnership.

"Answer, answer," Clare whispered, crouching over the handset, no longer picturing Richard sleeping—he would have picked up the phone by now. Maybe he was down the hall, trying to figure out how to use the fax machine, or perhaps in his private bathroom, where he couldn't hear the phone ringing. Eventually his voice mail kicked in, informing her that he was either on the phone or away from his desk.

"Richard," she said. "I'm sorry, but I seem to have forgotten if you have a meeting tonight. Do you?" She stopped and squeezed her eyes shut. She sounded like an idiot. Why didn't these machines have a "back up and redo" mechanism? "Please call."

She dialed Richard's car phone. The melodic baritone recording told her that the cellular customer she was trying to reach was "not available at this time." Maybe Marty, Richard's friend and law partner, would know where he was. But there were no listings for Martin Berg, or M. Berg, in Calabasas; his number would be unlisted, of course. Pacing beside the pool now, Clare called Richard's office number again, this time following his instructions for reaching his administrative assistant, Diana. Her phone rang and rang, then Diana's mincy little voice explained that she was "unable to take your call right now."

Clare went inside and slowly put the phone back in its kitchen wall cradle. She had run out of people to call.

CHAPTER TWO

WHEN THE BUZZING STARTED, RICHARD THOUGHT THE VOICES WERE RETURNING, but then Maya asked if he was going to answer his phone, and he knew he had misunderstood. No voices, only his phone. He reached into his jacket pocket and turned it off, then nodded his thanks as the waiter poured two glasses from the second bottle of Puligny-Montrachet.

"This is so nice of you," Maya Eastman said, "taking me out to dinner."

"But it's nothing!" Richard said. "I just need a little more …" What was it he needed? "… you know, stuff so I could finish up your trust papers."

He needed to slow down. His motor was speeding and the words were coming too fast, piling up against each other.

Maya frowned. "But when you called you said you wanted to get my take on the news conference about my divorce—how you dealt with the media."

Jesus. Is that what he told her?

"That, too. You said you watched it. How'd I do?"

"You were great. Just great."

She must have known that sounded feeble, for she added, "You said just enough but not too much."

Richard agreed. He knew how to handle the media, for sure. "The camera loves you," Phil had said, trying to convince him he should be the firm's spokesman for the Eastman-Barone divorce. Wentworth was such a jerk, trying to sound like a fucking filmmaker.

"Is there some reason you're worried about it? Is that why you called me?"

If he told her the truth, she'd think he was crazy. This morning, when the voices told him to turn right, not left, at the Kanan Road entrance to The 101, he knew with absolute certainty that he was supposed to go to Santa Monica. And when he got to the Third Street Promenade, as directed, the voices told him to call Maya.

"Richard?" Maya touched his hand.

Had he been talking to himself? He smiled and she smiled right back at him. That was good. She wasn't looking at him as if he'd done anything weird.

She raised her eyebrows. "The news conference?"

He waved his hand, swatting away the question. "No, no. It went fine. No fallout from Barry. And in a few months, you'll be rid of him forever."

Maya ducked her head in that appealing gesture she used to such good effect on *Days of Eternal Love*. She was beautiful in the way that hundreds—maybe thousands—of young women were in Los Angeles: blond, tanned, toned and, of course, well endowed up front. That her beautiful breasts were most likely surgically enhanced didn't matter at all. Richard sipped his wine and wondered if she was trying to seduce him. Not out of the question.

Maya tilted her head back, shaking her hair away from her face. "Aren't the stars lovely?"

Michael's was one of his favorite restaurants and tonight it was perfect. The wine was cold and delicious. The breezes from Santa Monica harbor took the edge off the heat, the voices hadn't returned, and he was safe, here on the restaurant's patio. The stars overhead shimmered and the wine glasses caught their light, filling the patio with a million fireflies: pure magic! He signaled the waiter for another bottle.

"Oh, not for me," Maya said

Richard ignored her protestations; he didn't need her help drinking another bottle. He tugged at his left ear, which was suddenly abuzz with static.

Maybe the voices were trying to reach him and couldn't get through. His leg started jumping. If only he could slow down.

"Is something the matter?" Maya asked.

Could she hear it, too? He wanted to ask her, but he doubted that she'd understand. Trust no one, a voice said then, coming through quite clearly.

"You look upset."

Richard gave her one of his brightest smiles. "I couldn't be better."

~

The coyotes yipping in the hills woke Clare at 12:30 a.m. Above the rattle of wind in the palms, she could hear packs of them in the surrounding landscape taking up the chant, until the whole circle of mountains that formed the Conejo Valley was filled with their chittering and howls. Moonlight shone through the window onto their bed to the place beside her, smooth and cold, where Richard should have lain. Clare reached out her hand and touched the spot where she usually slung her arm over him.

"Richard, please," she whispered, "please come home."

She picked up the phone to make sure the line wasn't dead, then slipped on her robe and crept down the hall to the boys' bedrooms. Adam slept cradling his teddy bear, an old habit he renewed since the move to Los Angeles. In the front bedroom, Matt was sprawled diagonally across his bed, tangled in a cotton blanket. One long, hairy leg stuck out from under the covering; she reached out and touched it. When had he developed those knotted muscles in his calves? She pulled the blanket up to cover his shoulders, and in his sleep Matt batted her hand away. He had done that even as a baby, when his hands were chubby and smooth, when the gesture had seemed cute.

Downstairs in the kitchen, she chose the non-emergency police number. It was probably foolish even to make the call. No, the dispatcher told her, there were no reports of automobile accidents between Encino, where Richard worked, and Agave Hills, where they lived. And though it seemed absurd to confine her inquiries to one twenty-odd-mile stretch of The 101—Los Angeles was so vast, he could be anywhere—she didn't know what else to ask.

Agave Hills lay one ridge west of the San Fernando Valley and a mountain range north of the west side of Los Angeles. It was a small city whose core was three strip malls, a town populated by a citizenry so scrubbed and white, so ostentatiously prosperous and determinedly upstanding, that nothing as unpleasant as tragedy could ever touch them. Though of course it had, for this very summer, the summer of 1995, O.J. Simpson was on trial for the murders of his wife and Ron Goldman, the son of a local resident. That tragedy hit home in Agave, but in a peculiar way, with people claiming whatever connection they could to the Goldmans: they went to the same temple, sat in a neighboring booth at the Oak Tree, knew a girl who had dated Ron in high school—as if any link to the tragedy were a talisman, a way to ward off sorrow from one's own family. But Agave Hills had its share of tragedies: in June one high school boy was fatally stabbed and another wounded by two classmates; a man just down the street had gone berserk only a week before, shooting at his neighbors from behind his living room sofa.

"Will you take his license plate, in case anything turns up?" Clare asked.

"Yes. What's the number, please?" The dispatcher sounded pressed for time. Clare realized there were true emergencies out there, calls the dispatcher needed to tend to.

"It's not a number, it's a name. You know, a vanity plate?"

"I know what a vanity plate is," the dispatcher replied.

"It's 'TrstMe,'" Clare said, making a face in the dark. "He's a trust attorney, so it's kind of like advertising." Shut up, she told herself—the dispatcher doesn't care. "Will you call me if he's been in an accident?"

"Ma'am." The dispatcher was patient now that the conversation was ending. "It's better if you call us. But give it some time."

Clare ran her hand over the plastic relief map of Los Angeles she had bought last week, trying to familiarize herself with the terrain. She touched the little ridge of hills that separates the Conejo and San Fernando valleys. At the top of the ridge was Calabasas, where Marty Berg lived. She slid her index finger across the broad, asphalt plain of the valley eastward to Studio City, skidded over the Hollywood Hills, down onto the flat expanse of central Los Angeles, south to where the little bump of Palos Verdes emerges above Long Beach, then down onto Orange County. Where in this enormous, alien landscape could Richard be?

~◦

Richard woke to the sound of trees screaming. For a moment, he didn't know where he was and then it came back to him—the dinner at Michael's, the three bottles of wine, Maya. He could hear her breathing, feel the heat of her body inches from his. Jesus. He leapt out of bed.

The bedside clock read 3:00 a.m. Tuesday already. He pressed his palms against his ears to muffle the sound of the trees, but it didn't help. They were taunting him. "Stop it!" he cried. "Shut up!"

"What's the matter?" Maya sat up in bed, her breasts silvery in the light from the street lamp. "Richard, what is it?" She held out her hand to him.

"Don't touch me," he said. "Get away from me." He backed against the wall, as far as he could get from her in the small room. "You lured me here to this, this—cabin. This isn't your house. You live in Brentwood, I know that. You're holding me here until they come and get me."

"Richard, don't you remember? I'm staying away from my house in case Barry tries to come after me. This place belongs to one of the girls I work with. It's a safe house."

"You're lying," Richard shouted. "You know they're after me."

Maya reached for the bottle on the bedside table. "Here, let me get you a drink." Maybe a little Stoli would knock him out. Richard took the glass from her, sniffed it, then drank the alcohol in two fast gulps.

"Promise me," Richard said. "Promise you won't tell anyone you've seen me."

"I promise."

"If you tell anyone, they'll come after you, too."

"Who will come after me? Are you talking about Barry?"

Richard's hand shook as he poured himself another glass. "I can't tell you. It's for your protection. Just keep this to yourself. Don't tell anybody you've seen me or that you've been with me, and no one will hurt you."

"I won't tell a soul," Maya promised.

Judging it was safe, she moved closer and took Richard's hand.

"Come on," she whispered, easing him into the bed beside her. "Relax." She moved closer, pressing her breasts to his chest as she slid her hand between his legs.

Richard groaned. "No," he said. But he didn't mean it. The pressure inside him was building. Any minute his brain would blow apart, fragments of flesh and bone flying across the room. He wasn't Richard Stone; he was the sum of overwhelming forces that were propelling him towards oblivion. He rolled on top of her, the full length and weight of his body pressing her down into the mattress. He pushed into her and heard, as if from a distance, Maya asking him to wait for her, but he didn't slow down. He couldn't. He collapsed onto his elbows and then flopped onto his back beside her.

She lay still as he stroked her face, wiping her tears with his hand. "I'm sorry. I'm sorry. I didn't mean ... Are you all right?"

"It's okay," Maya said. "Don't worry." She moved his hand away from her face. "Let's go to sleep." She turned on her side and spooned her body into his. Richard wrapped his arms around her and pulled her close.

"Remember," he murmured, nuzzling her neck. "You haven't seen me."

When Maya fell asleep, snoring softly, Richard's panic returned. The trees started up again, harsher this time: calling him by name, accusing him of assault, of rape. He needed to get away from here. They were after him, he was sure. He needed to move fast.

CHAPTER THREE

DIANA WASN'T IN WHEN CLARE CALLED AT 9:00 ON TUESDAY MORNING, NOR WAS she at her desk when she called again at 9:15. Clare finally reached her at 9:20. No, Diana reported, she knew of no out-of-town trips, but she had been out sick yesterday, so maybe Mr. Stone's schedule had changed. Would Mrs. Stone like to talk to Mr. Berg or Mr. Wentworth?

"Mr. Berg."

"Hold on."

Marty Berg was a college friend of Richard's. They had shared a dormitory suite at Yale in the days when colleges didn't try to match roommates with similar interests. They could hardly have been more different: Marty Berg from Brooklyn, the first in his family to go to college, and Richard Stone of Sainsbury, Connecticut, member of a Yankee clan that had resided there for more than two hundred years. Yet it was Marty who stayed in New England for law school and Richard who opted for Boalt Hall in Berkeley, California. After he graduated, Marty, too, settled in California but in the south, in Los Angeles, which he loved because of the weather. Last December, on a business trip north to the Bay Area, Marty called Richard and invited him and Clare to dinner.

"Why do you suppose he wants me to come?" Clare asked as Richard sped across the Bay Bridge. She braced herself against the dashboard as he wove the Lexus in and out of traffic. God, he was reckless.

"He mentioned that he and Jodie have separated again. He probably wants to see a couple who's happily married." Richard reached over and massaged the back of her neck.

~⬯

It wasn't happy marriages Marty wanted to talk about, though. Over dinner, Marty explained that he and Phil Wentworth, his partner, were looking for a third partner for their San Fernando Valley law firm.

"You'd love it," Marty said, his voice too loud for the restaurant. "We have a premier practice. Lawyers to the stars." He held his hands up as if he were introducing an act. "TV stars," he added.

When they had finished dessert, Marty leaned back in his chair. "We really want you, Richard," he said. "We need a trust attorney. All our clients have more money than they know what to do with. They need tax planning, trusts set up to protect their assets. It's half our practice now, and I have to refer it out. We need somebody with your reputation. What is it the *San Francisco Chronicle* calls you? The Titan of Trusts?"

Richard laughed. "I got lucky."

~⬯

"This wasn't a setup, right? You didn't already tell Marty you'd take that job?" Clare asked as they made their way out of San Francisco through the fog.

"I haven't—I wouldn't—make any commitment to him unless you agree."

"Promise?"

"Trust me," Richard answered, leaning across the gear shift to kiss her before the light changed.

The party the firm held to lure Richard into their partnership was at Phil Wentworth's Encino estate—"A real spread," Richard observed, taking Clare's hand and leading her across the broad, slightly sloping lawn. Though it was late January, the temperature was mild and the sunlight so bright and white that Clare stopped and felt among the tissue crumbs and furry mints in the depths of her purse for sunglasses. At the foot of the yard, under a gazebo large enough to be called a pavilion, Clare could see fifteen or twenty people gathered, wine glasses in hand. One tall man with a full head of white hair broke away from the crowd and approached, teeth gleaming and hand held out in greeting.

"I'm Phil Wentworth, and you must be Clare," he said, as if the two facts were linked. Clare smiled and nodded, holding her hand out for the hearty grasp she expected but didn't receive. Phil Wentworth's hand was cool and lifeless. She drew her hand away quickly, then felt the pressure of Richard's palm on her back, willing her to make a good impression.

"Phil! Philip!" A small woman with bright, spiky hair flapped her hand at him. "We're waiting for you!"

Phil shrugged. "Maria," he said. "My wife. She keeps me organized." Clare smiled, as she was expected to do, and turned to Richard. He cleared his throat.

"We'd love to meet her," Richard said.

Phil led them the rest of the distance across the lawn to Maria. Up closer, his wife's face had the taut, too-smooth look of plastic surgery. Clare held her smile through Maria's quick, unconcealed appraisal of her hair, makeup and clothes. They were so competitive, these LA women. What was Richard getting them into?

"I'm so glad you could come," Maria said at last, smiling tightly. Then she turned to Richard. "Phil is absolutely thrilled."

Maria was pulled away from them by another woman, and Clare accepted a glass of Sauvignon Blanc from a tray held by a young Mexican man in white shirt and black pants, pausing only slightly to consider if she should go with the mineral water. She turned to Richard, close beside her, and there was only the tiniest flicker of concern in his eyes.

"You're doing great," he whispered, leaning close so his lips were against her ear, his face in her hair. She got goosebumps from his touch, even though it must have been nearly eighty degrees in the Valley.

"What is Phil 'thrilled' about exactly?" she asked.

"That's just LA bullshit," Richard said. "I already told you. I haven't—I wouldn't—make any commitment to them unless you agree."

"Promise?"

Clare was desperate at the thought of living in Los Angeles. The facelifts, the fake breasts, the year-round tans. It wasn't real. It was just like its stereotype—plastic. That's what she and Richard would have called it in the sixties; to be "plastic" was the ultimate insult. Though Los Angeles was also, in the geological sense, plastic. That was the frightening thing about it. It was constantly changing, for eons rearranging itself by earthquake, fire, flood, erosion and landslide—ruthless natural forces in an unnatural setting of vast green lawns and cement-lined riverbeds.

In the end, Clare acquiesced to his wishes, as she suspected he knew she would. She vowed to try her best in LA, to try to be swept away on the riptide of Richard's enthusiasm, his contagious excitement for the next grand stage of their lives.

~

"Berg," Marty barked into the phone, startling her.

"It's Clare Stone."

"Hey!" He sounded delighted. "What's up?"

"It's nothing, probably." She went through a recitation of last night's vigil, waiting for Marty to recall some out-of-town trip that was not on Richard's calendar.

"He never mentioned anything at our partners' meeting Friday."

"What about yesterday?"

"He wasn't here yesterday," Marty said. He paused, and Clare felt her heart knocking against her chest wall.

"At least I don't think he was. Hold on. Let me check with Phil."

"Oh no, oh no," Clare whispered.

"Clare?" Marty was back on the line; she could hear him tapping something against his desk. "Phil agrees he wasn't here yesterday." He stopped tapping. "We need to call the police."

Clare heard him through static, his voice drowned out by an intense buzzing in her head—the sound of cicadas, so loud it made her nauseated—and she slowly slid to the kitchen floor, pressing her back against a cupboard for support.

"Clare?"

"Just a minute," she gasped, normal breathing failing her.

She should file a missing persons report with the police, Marty said, and he would call one of the firm's private investigators and get him on Richard's trail right away.

Go to the police? She wanted to ask Richard what she should do, but of course he wasn't here. It was automatic to think of turning to him for help, a habit of nearly twenty years. She didn't want to go to the police. Reporting Richard as missing—missing!—made it real. Until now, she was frightened, sure, but there was always the possibility that she had been distracted, missing something he had told her.

"Clare?" Marty was saying. "Can you hear me? There was no business trip."

"I heard." She clicked the phone off.

CHAPTER FOUR

THE LOST HILLS SHERIFF'S STATION HUDDLED IN THE SUNBURNT FOOTHILLS between The 101 and the Santa Monica Mountains. An effort had been made to coordinate the building with the landscape: its green corrugated roof echoed the color of the dusty foliage of the surrounding scrub oaks and the red brick exterior complemented the rusty adobe soil. Inside, it was just like any other governmental office: a long counter and glass partitions kept the public at a remove from the uniformed men and women who chatted easily in the distance, ignoring the cluster of people waiting.

Clare fought back the urge to shriek for attention; it wouldn't hurry them and would make her look crazy. Shifting from one shaky leg to the other, she scratched at a piece of torn cuticle and waited. While she stood, two uniformed men came into the room.

"You waiting for someone?" the older of the two asked her.

"I need to file a missing persons report."

He rapped his knuckles on the counter and a young woman appeared from behind a partition.

"Chris'll take care of you," he said, leaving.

The woman's name tag identified her as Deputy Szabo. She listened to Clare's explanation of Richard's absence, then reached under the counter for a thick tablet, tearing off a form from the top. In Los Angeles, Clare noted, missing persons report forms came in bulk.

The form was basic: today's date, age, date of birth, height, weight, hair and eye color, and "gang."

September 26, 1995; forty-five; March 30, 1950; six feet tall; 175 pounds; light brown hair; brown eyes.

Clare put the pen down. "Light brown" didn't begin to describe Richard's hair. She loved his hair, dark blond shot through with rusty highlights. And his eyes—not merely brown but a particular shade of brown, the color of chocolate with flecks of gold. The beauty of her husband, of his spirit, couldn't be captured by the ordinary language of a police report. But it didn't matter. If the police found him, it wouldn't be because the color of his eyes changed with the light. Under "Gang" she wrote "N/A." The next box was titled "Record Type" and included Runaway Juvenile, Voluntary Missing Adult, Parental/Family Abduction, Stranger Abduction, Catastrophe, Sexual Exploitation Suspected, Lost, and Unknown Circumstances. Could Richard be a "Voluntary Missing Adult?" Or was his disappearance simply a "Catastrophe?" She checked "Unknown Circumstances."

"When you search for missing people," Clare asked, sliding the form across the counter, "do you put a notice in the newspapers?"

"We don't do anything for the first seventy-two hours," the deputy said, "unless there's a reason to suspect foul play. Is there?" She looked at the form. "'Didn't come home. Didn't go to work.' That's it?"

"Well, yes. I can't imagine why he wouldn't show up for work and why he wouldn't come home."

Deputy Szabo's expression softened and Clare thought how she must appear: an anxious housewife with a roaming husband, a suburban cliché.

She flushed. "That is, of course, I can imagine why, but it would be so out of character ..."

Deputy Szabo nodded, not meeting her eyes. The officer who had helped her came back into the office. "Maybe Captain McVay can help you."

"What's happening?" he asked.

"Missing person. This woman's husband."

22

He motioned to Clare. "Come on in here, Mrs. ...."—he glanced at the form—"Stone," he said.

He led Clare to a glassed-in office. The sun coming through the window gave the illusion of warmth despite the chill of the building's air conditioning. She noted the predictable personal items on his desk among the government-issue office supplies—a picture of a smiling boy in a football uniform and a group portrait of a much younger, luxuriantly sideburned Captain McVay with a pretty, slope-shouldered wife and two blond children. He nodded at Clare.

"Tell me about it."

Clasping her hands together tightly in her lap to stop their shaking, she told him how Richard had not come home Monday night and Marty's news that Richard had not been at work that day, either. The officer nodded and made a few notes on the form.

"Has this happened before, Mrs. Stone?"

"No."

"No womanizing?"

"Never."

"Has your husband been under any unusual stress lately?"

Clare frowned. "No, no more than the rest of us."

"Meaning what?" the captain asked.

"It's just that we moved away from all our friends. My husband started a new job as a partner in a law firm, and we have a new house."

"And that's in ..." He scanned the form. "Agave Hills? Grey Rock Road?"

She saw McVay's eyes stray to her wedding ring, a two-carat brilliant-cut diamond that Richard had given her on their fifteenth anniversary. In Alameda it had been ostentatious; in Los Angeles it was puny.

"The move's been hard," she said.

He nodded and his eyes lost their focus, looking past her to the windows beyond her shoulder, toward the freeway. He was not impressed, Clare could see, with the miseries of a wealthy attorney whose only tragedy was a fancy new job and a big house to go with it. She felt like she was losing the deputy and with that all hope of finding Richard.

She leaned forward, pinching the edge of his desk with her fingertips. "You've got to believe me. Richard would never leave us like this. Something has happened to him."

"Well." McVay laced his freckled fingers together. "In the great majority of cases, these things resolve themselves. People turn up."

"Why do they disappear?"

The officer shrugged. "Lots of reasons. Sometimes they just forget to say they'll be gone. Other times, they go on a bender." He shifted in the chair a little, wincing. "And other times ..." He held his hands up, raising his eyebrows and shoulders simultaneously. "Who knows?"

"And if he doesn't show up?" Clare asked. "What do you do then?"

"After seventy-two hours we put out a bulletin, circulate his description and the license plate of his car, and let the press know."

"But something has happened to him, I'm sure. Every hour we wait ..."

"Let's give it a day or two. You don't know this, but I see it all the time." He rolled his chair back and stood. "It will work itself out."

He patted her shoulder as he opened the office door.

"He'll turn up okay, Mrs. Stone," the captain said. "You just wait."

Clare stood at the doorway of the family room where Matt and Adam were watching *Forrest Gump* for what must have been the tenth time. She waited another moment, poised on the divide between their ignorance and her knowledge. She had to tell them Richard was missing; Matt had already asked when he was coming home and she'd said she was "waiting for him." She owed them more than the technical truth. On the screen, Forrest ran across a succession of American landscapes.

"Boys, I need to talk to you about Dad." Both Matt and Adam looked up. "Turn off the TV," she told Matt.

"What's wrong?" he asked, frowning as he pressed the remote control.

"Where is he?" Adam asked, his voice quavering.

"I'm not sure," she answered, circling around and pulling an ottoman over so she could face both of them, side by side in their favorite comfy chairs. She clasped her hands in her lap so the boys wouldn't see she was trembling. "That's why I need to talk to you."

"Is he all right?" Matt asked.

"We don't know yet."

"Who is 'we'?" Matt sounded angry, and Adam was starting to cry. Clare reached over and pulled him to her as she spoke.

"Daddy's partners at the office. I talked to them this morning, because Dad apparently didn't have a business trip last night." Adam opened his arms and knelt beside her with his head across her lap. She stroked his hair. "And?" Matt's voice was louder now.

"And no one knows where he went, but Marty says he has his briefcase with him, so he must have had some meetings, but just to be on the safe side, I did talk to the police"—at this point Adam cried out, and she hugged him to her—"and they're looking for Daddy, too. Everybody's doing everything they can to find him."

Matt shook his head. "He's not missing," he said. "You know how you never remember anything. Dad told you where he was going and you forgot."

"I didn't forget."

"Will we still start school Thursday?" Adam asked. School. She had forgotten about school.

"Yes. Of course."

Adam sat back on his haunches and wiped his eyes with one hand. "But what if Dad calls and no one's here?" he asked.

"I'll be here. I'll take you to school, and I'll take my cell phone with me so I won't miss Dad's call."

Matt got up and strode outside, his fists clenched, and Clare followed, bracing herself for the shouting match that would undoubtedly ensue. Instead she found him kneeling on the patio's pebbled concrete, clutching Merlin to his chest.

"I didn't forget, Matty," she told him again. "Dad didn't tell me where he was going." When she put her hand on his back, he buried his face in the cat's fur. She knelt beside him and wrapped her son and the cat in her arms, and this time Matt didn't push her away.

CHAPTER FIVE

RICHARD'S DESK WAS ORDERLY. CLARE THOUGHT OF HIM AS MESSY ABOUT HOUSE-hold matters—coffee cups growing mold by the computer, scraps of paper with little scribbled notes by his favorite chair—but his desk had always been a model of organization. Leather-trimmed blotter squarely in the middle, pen holder neatly arranged at the top right. Stationery in the right-hand drawer, pens in the middle. Financial information—checkbooks and files on the left.

Clare examined all the records. Nothing. She recognized every name, could identify almost every credit card receipt. It was all old stuff, as if he hadn't touched it for months, just unpacked and never went back to the desk. Next she looked through their checkbook. Again, there was nothing unusual: groceries, something for $76.13 at Bullock's, a check to Circuit City for a new VCR after their old one died. These were the records of a normal life, nothing that would explain what had happened when a man leaves for work and doesn't come home.

"Remember this, Mom?" Adam surprised her, holding a photo album he must have pulled from one of the boxes. "Remember our condo in the Caymans? How we watched all those cooking shows when it was too hot to go outside?"

Clare put her hand on Adam's bony back and peered over his shoulder at the smiling, sunlit photo of the four of them on a bench, shaded by an exotic tree growing right out of the sand, almost at the edge of the ocean. The boys looked so small and she and Richard so young.

"Sure, I remember."

Richard liked to surprise her with gifts. She loved the excitement she felt when he would appear suddenly by her side, his eyes shining and his hands behind his back, hiding a piece of jewelry or airline tickets. He'd tell her to "pack light—it'll be hot" and "bring the passports." Then, early next morning, they would take a cab to the Oakland Airport and lift off over San Francisco Bay, the fog and damp receding below them, not stopping until they were in a country of sweet smells, crimson vines and steel drums.

~

Tuesday night. The second night he didn't come home. She didn't know what to do with herself, so she kept moving. That was the only thing she believed would help. The boys had been fed; the dishwasher was loaded. She had eaten a few teaspoons of yogurt while standing at the counter. She couldn't sit still. At least the yogurt was nourishing and could be swallowed without chewing. Chewing was out of the question.

It was that in-between time in the Southern California latitudes: late in the day but still light, neither day nor night. Normally—if there had been such a thing as "normal" since they'd moved here—she would be making dinner, waiting for the sound of the door and the music that signaled Richard's arrival. She wiped down the kitchen counters automatically, her chest weighted with the increasing conviction that Richard would never again swing his car into their garage, stereo blaring.

Taking the portable phone out to the patio, she settled into one of the chairs and Merlin leapt into her lap, kneading at her thighs and purring. She stroked his fur absently as she dialed her mother. The message on Audrey's answering machine referred callers with an emergency to contact Joan, Audrey's best friend. Interrupted in the middle of a bridge game, Joan told Clare that her mother was gone until the following Monday on a cruise with Chuck, whom Clare still thought of as her mother's new husband even though they'd been married for ten years.

It had been a relief at first, when Audrey announced that she had found a "nice new friend." Now she wouldn't have to feel so responsible for her mother's happiness. Chuck was an avid golfer, the owner of a gigantic, deluxe recreational vehicle and a member of an RV touring group. Every year, it seemed, Audrey and Chuck would go for months-long vacations, traveling in RV caravans with other retirees, stopping to play golf here, tennis somewhere else. Though her mother didn't seem to care much for golf, claiming she played only "to keep Chuck company," she had taken to tennis with surprising intensity. When Clare, Richard and the boys visited them at one of their RV encampments near San Diego, Clare was surprised to find Audrey, her leathery legs tanned and muscular, lounging in tennis whites with several similarly clad women, laughing and drinking gin-and-tonics before noon. It didn't seem right, somehow, for her mother to be having such a good time.

She knew she should call Richard's father, but how could she tell him his only child had disappeared? She worried about the effect the news would have on Nathaniel Stone's health. He seemed more fragile lately, his voice reedier when she talked to him on the phone. He was a wonderful man, the dream of a father she never had. There was no way she could burden him with this terrible information. She would wait another day.

She called Richard's cell phone again, but he didn't answer.

~⊙

The phone's ring startled Richard and he jerked the wheel, unintentionally crossing the center line. He corrected immediately but still earned the blast of a horn as a Mercedes convertible shot past, its driver punching the sky with his middle finger. Richard tossed the cell phone out the window and watched it bounce on the Pacific Coast Highway, then shatter.

He checked the rear view mirror to see if he was being followed. He needed a drink badly. Maybe he could find one in Ventura, some seedy tavern where he wouldn't risk running into anyone he knew. His leg jiggled involuntarily. It might be difficult to find a place where no one would recognize him. He'd been all over the news last week, answering reporters' questions about Maya Eastman's divorce. He gripped the steering wheel harder. He didn't want to think about Maya.

In Ventura, on a bleak street of used-clothing shops and vacant storefronts, he found a dark bar that smelled of beer and last night's cigarettes. The few patrons hunched over their drinks barely glanced at him. After a couple shots of Smirnoff—below his standards but the only vodka they had on hand—his nerves began to settle. This was good. This was good. He would devise a way to evade his pursuers. Okay. First, he needed to get rid of this suit. Of course! The second-hand stores! It was wonderful the way he knew instinctively that this bar, on this street of stores, was precisely the place to go. He rubbed his chin. It would be several days before he'd have much of a beard, but that was okay. What else to do? What else, what else?

Clare lay in bed listening to the song of a mockingbird somewhere outside in the dark, running through its repertoire of imitations over and over while she ran through the possible explanations for Richard's disappearance: death, injury, kidnapping.

Or Richard could be with another woman. That was obviously what Captain McVay thought. An old story. Clare shifted in the bed, pulling the sheet tightly against her shoulder. There was his secretary, Diana. Forget it. Female attorneys he met in the course of his work? She turned over on her back and brushed her hair away from her face. He wouldn't risk losing his whole life—her, the kids, the house—for another woman. Or would he? Her father had done that—left his family, just walked out of their lives. Men did it all the time. But not Richard.

She sat up at the sound of the ringing phone.

"Sorry to call so late." It was Marty's voice. "I just got out of a meeting."

Clare could hear a distant siren and the steady ding-ding-ding of the seat belt alarm as Marty spoke. She imagined him barreling down Ventura Boulevard in his Mercedes, honking at anyone driving at the speed limit, changing CD tracks and adjusting the volume.

"I wanted to let you know we hired a private investigator. He'll contact you tomorrow."

"But I already went to the police, like you said."

"The cops don't have the time for this. They don't see it as urgent, and we need to act right away. Trust me, I know about this stuff."

"I'm not sure ..." Clare said.

"And there's something else you should do. Check your bank accounts, your savings—anything that Richard would have access to—and see if he's withdrawn any money. The investigator will follow the credit card trails; you deal with the banks."

"I'll do that first thing tomorrow," Clare promised. "Anything else?"

"Listen, I don't want to upset you, but yeah. We need—I need—to consider," Marty took a deep breath. "Richard's a trustee of a lot of people's money. We need to be sure he hasn't tampered with any of it."

"But Marty," Clare protested, "he'd never do anything like that."

"It's for his protection as well as our clients'. We're having accountants go through all Richard's files tomorrow. I'm just warning you. When attorneys drop out of sight, the first thing the police do is look at their sources of money. If there's something we don't know about Richard—some problem he had that would explain why he disappeared—the money might be a clue."

"Richard wouldn't steal from his clients."

"I'll call you tomorrow," Marty said. "You'll be hearing from the investigator. Gotta go."

"Wait! What's his name?"

"Moe Billingsley. Oh yeah. Another thing. Tomorrow the *LA Times* and the other local papers are going to run stories and Richard's picture. We need to get the word out, so people will recognize him. He's out there somewhere, I'm sure of it."

CHAPTER SIX

WEDNESDAY MORNING'S *LOS ANGELES TIMES* RAN A SHORT ARTICLE ON PAGE B4 OF its "Valley Focus" section under the headline "Agave Hills Man Reported Missing."

> *Richard Stone, 45, a San Fernando Valley attorney, was reported missing Tuesday morning. According to police, Stone did not show up for work in Encino as expected Monday morning, and did not return home that evening. Stone is 6 ft., 175 lb., with light brown hair and brown eyes and was last seen driving a black 1994 Lexus LS400 sedan, license plate "TrstMe." County Sheriff's Captain Joseph McVay asks that anyone who has any information about Stone's whereabouts call the Lost Hills Sheriff's Station.*

The local paper, the *Thousand Oaks Star*, ran a nearly identical article as well as the law firm's photo of Richard at the bottom of its front page.

Jannie, her only candidate for friendship in the neighborhood, was the first to call that morning. The week the Stones moved in, she drove up to the house and introduced herself, offering to take the kids off Clare's hands while she unpacked. Clare had seen her twice since in the grocery line at Von's. Both times they had vowed to get together for coffee, but it hadn't happened.

"Clare? I saw the papers. Are you all right?"

"No."

Merlin had settled himself on the *Thousand Oaks Star*, exactly on top of the photograph of Richard's face. Clare scooped him off the counter with her free arm.

"Sorry," Jannie was saying. "Stupid question. Look, why don't I take your guys to the beach with me today? Tell them to bring their boogie boards. We'll go to Zuma Beach."

When Jannie knocked at the door later, Matt and Adam appeared at the top of the stairs. Matt had his long-suffering face on.

"Have a good time, guys," Clare said, willing Matt to be civil. He wouldn't meet her eyes.

"I'll have them back by four," Jannie promised.

~

It seemed unfair that in the midst of losing her husband she should need groceries, but she was low on toothpaste, the boys had finished the last of the milk with their cereal this morning, and she needed something to feed them tonight. Clare sped through the aisles of Von's supermarket, keeping up for once with the impatient pace of the other shoppers. Los Angeles, famous for being "laid back," was full of people in a perpetual hurry, always anxious to be someplace else. The produce—escarole-green, eggplant-purple, crookneck-yellow—sparkled unnaturally in neatly arranged bins. The lights of the store shimmered just enough to be irritating. She stood behind a woman in the checkout line who wore black spandex shorts and a sports bra, showing off her tan, taut midriff and high, rounded glutes. The woman's ponytail protruded through the gap in the back of her baseball cap, which sported a Fox Television logo. Mirrored sunglasses, big breasts, thin, muscular upper arms and perfect, perfect makeup: a dark brown outline carefully drawn around a puffy, chocolate-colored mouth. So trendy, Clare thought. So 1995. The woman turned, gazed at Clare for a second and then turned away, sighing audibly and clicking her manicured fingernails on the rim of her cart handle. As the checkstand conveyor emptied, she transferred her groceries to the belt: two liters of Pellegrino, a jar of melatonin, plastic bags of peaches, plums, and kiwis.

Outside in the parking lot, the sunlight and its reflection off the asphalt temporarily blinded Clare, and she held her hand out, trying to steady herself against the dizzying wave that rushed over her. When she found her sunglasses at last—perched on top of her head—she looked around as shoppers rushed past, intent on their grocery lists or pushing heavy carts towards their cars. Her husband was missing, had been missing for three days, and people were going about their daily lives as if nothing was wrong.

~⌒

Steve Rosado was waiting in his truck in front of their house, talking on his cell phone, when Clare returned from the grocery store. He folded the telephone, slipped it into his shirt pocket, and swung his lean, muscular body down from the truck's high cab.

"Hi," he said, holding out his hand. "Am I early? I thought we'd said ten o'clock."

"I'm sorry. I forgot," Clare responded. "There's been so much …"

"I won't bother you, I promise," he interrupted, holding one hand up. "Just show me where you want the pergola."

Clare followed him up the walk. "Pergola? What are you talking about?"

"The pergola your husband said you wanted."

"You talked to my husband? After we saw you Saturday?"

"Yeah." Steve looked puzzled. "Why?"

"My husband's missing," Clare said. "When did you talk to him?"

"Missing."

"When did you talk to him?" she repeated.

"Let's see," he gazed upwards, squinting. "Sunday night." He nodded, as if to himself. "Yeah, it was Sunday night." He frowned. "It was kind of strange. I mean, he called so late."

"Tell me everything you remember."

They sat together on the cool bricks of the front steps, shaded by the evergreen camphor trees that flanked the walk.

"He called real late for a customer," Steve said. "It was almost midnight."

Midnight. She ran through the events of the evening: Richard had left to pick up some documents at his office after dinner, returning after she had gone to bed and waking her so they could make love—if making love was what you could call it. There were times—Sunday night was one of them— when she was beside the point. That night and most of the weekend was ruled by whatever Richard wanted. And what he wanted more than anything was sex. But even sex didn't calm Richard that night. He was restless. Around midnight she heard him prowling around the kitchen, mumbling. He must have been on the phone with Steve. Every hour or two he would come to bed, pull her close to him and try to sleep. She doubted he closed his eyes for a full hour all night.

"Your husband said he'd been thinking about it and that you definitely wanted a pergola. He told me to go ahead and design it."

"How did he sound?"

"Well, he was, you know, enthusiastic. Lots of energy." Steve shook his head. "But most clients don't do that. Call at midnight." He was silent for a few moments, then turned to Clare.

"So I guess you don't want me to do the landscaping, then."

"I don't know what to do."

Steve nodded. "Sure. I understand."

"The garden—it's really important to Richard, but I just can't think about it right now. Not until he comes back." She turned her head away.

"Listen, "Steve said. "I've got plenty of time. Why don't I take some measurements and check out the light and shadows. No charge. Then when your husband comes back, you can decide if you want to go forward with the project or not."

Clare shrugged, then made an effort to pull herself together. "That's very nice of you."

Steve patted her back like she did for her boys when they were upset. It was a relief that he didn't say anything more, that he didn't try to tell her everything was going to be okay.

Barry Barone pressed his palms against the warm stucco wall, stretching his hamstrings while he waited for his heart rate to return to normal. Running was the only thing that made him feel really good these days, the only time he could focus on something other than Maya and what she'd done to him. Pushing off from the wall, he noticed how much better his biceps looked. He was nearly back in shape. Soon he'd return to boxing.

He tugged at the door of his apartment—since the quake last November everything had shifted—until it popped open and an air-conditioned breeze, stale and cool, washed over him. Apartments were cheap and easy to come by in Northridge; everyone was afraid to live here now. He remembered the solidity of the big mahogany door at Maya's house in Brentwood, so different from this hollow-core piece of crap. He hated Northridge, with its neglected streets and piles of lumber that used to be houses. He missed the Brentwood place, its cool tile floors, the swimming pool. The people who rented this apartment before him upped and left the day after the quake, he heard, leaving everything behind—furniture, dishes, clothes. Lots of people did weird things in the weeks and months after Northridge. Some of them, like the renters of his apartment, used the earthquake as an excuse to leave LA. Some people got married and some kicked their husbands out, like Maya did. It didn't take but a few shakes of the ground to wreck his life. He could have talked Maya into letting him stay if she hadn't hired those lawyers, Stone and Berg. They did this to him, offering a settlement so puny that all he could afford was this miserable place.

He poured a glass of orange juice and clicked on the TV. On the screen, Johnnie Cochran was pacing in front of the jury in a black knit cap, gesticulating, deep into his closing argument. Barry smiled. Like everyone he knew, Barry watched what the news called "The Trial of the Century" and chose sides. Most of the guys at the gym were African Americans and they believed O.J. was framed by the LAPD. All the white guys except Barry kept quiet but you could tell they thought O.J. did it. But Barry was different. Barry wanted O.J. to go free.

"He is not perfect," Cochran was saying. "He is not proud of some of the things he did. But they don't add up to murder."

"Yeah!" Barry shouted at the television. Cochran was right. No way was O.J. guilty. To Barry, though, it didn't matter. What mattered was that O.J.'s wife, ex-wife—whatever—had pushed him over the edge, taunting him with her new life, her life without him. So she got what she deserved. End of story. He was sorry that the trial was ending before he was ready to get back into training at the gym. He'd been watching it daily for months. Now how would he fill the long days? All he'd have to think about was Maya and her fucking lawyers.

Barry reached for the phone and dialed Stone's office, but at the sound of that secretary's voice—like fingernails on a blackboard—he clicked off.

Grunting as he pushed himself up from the couch, he grabbed the keys to the five-year-old black van Maya had not-so-graciously given him and wrestled into a track jacket. It was a good day to pay Stone a visit.

CHAPTER SEVEN

BEING THE WIFE OF A MISSING MAN WAS BECOMING AN OCCUPATION. LATER THAT morning Clare spent hours on the telephone, dealing with detail. That was okay. She had always liked detail. It was easy to get lost in it. She phoned their bank in Alameda, arranging to have their checking account closed and savings account frozen. She was humiliated at having to tell the bank manager that Richard had disappeared and that she had been advised to cut off any sources of money for him.

"It's just precautionary," she said. "No one suspects him of anything."

"Of course not."

She could tell he didn't believe her. By lunch time it would be all over town.

Clare returned to the study, to Richard's desk. She put her head down on its leather pad and breathed in; it smelled of him—his skin, his aftershave, even the particular pencils he preferred.

She sat up, tucked her hair behind her ears, and started searching through his desk again. This time, she pulled the drawers all the way out, to see if there was anything far in the back that she had missed. The first two small drawers on the right had nothing unusual—just note cards with envelopes and old postcards. At the back of the center drawer, though, banded together with the little instruction books that come with pocket calculators and other small electronic equipment, Clare found a picture of a woman she had never seen before. The woman was pretty and dark-haired, leaning on her elbow with her chin cupped in her hand, smiling at the camera. The photo looked as if it had been taken at some sort of conference; there were papers stacked to one side of her and water glasses on a tray beside a big pitcher. In the background were groups of people seated around similar-sized tables, with more papers and glasses. Behind the photograph was a piece of paper folded into a small rectangle. Both the photo and the note were well concealed in the bundle of booklets. The note was in a pretty, feminine hand—so different from her own crabbed script. It said, "Richard—you'll never know how much your caring means to me." It was signed with a single sinuous "S."

Making her way across the hall, Clare crawled into bed and curled into herself, pulling her knees to her chest and rocking gently. It was one thing to wonder if Richard was having an affair; it was another thing altogether to find that it was true. She didn't know how long she stayed in bed, feeling at a total loss, but after a while she called Marty and told him she needed to see him right away.

"No problem. Come on down."

"You'll have to tell me how to get there, to your office," Clare said.

"What do you mean?" Marty sounded puzzled.

"I've never driven to Encino. I've driven on the freeways only once down here." She could hear him snort and waited for some joke about needing to get out more. It was worse that the expected joke never came.

~○

She repeated Richard's driving warnings as she sped east towards the San Fernando Valley. Don't make eye contact with other drivers. If someone comes up behind you fast and close, signal to change lanes and do it immediately. If you can't keep up with the flow of traffic, get over to the far right lane and even then, drive as fast as you can. Don't get off the freeway unless you're sure where you are. Always bring a map. And a cell phone. Keep the windows up and the doors locked.

Clare wiped her palms on the lap of her skirt, one at a time so she could hang on to the wheel. She took a deep breath and leaned back in the seat. This wasn't so hard.

In LA, they added "The" to the freeway numbers, making them into something other than mere roads. People referred to The 101, The 405 and The 10 as if they were old friends. And there were odd touches: a stretch of The 101 near Encino was kept clean, a sign bragged, by Bette Midler.

"Have you seen her, Dad?" Adam asked, "by the side of the freeway?"

"Sure—but only very early. Ya gotta get up early to see Bette."

"What's she like?"

"You know—leopardskin tights and backless heels."

Matt, disgusted with Adam's question, laughed in spite of himself.

"And an orange vest," Richard concluded. "Bette's very safety conscious. She always wears her orange vest."

Richard was comfortable with the freeways; he had no trouble getting around. "It's easy to get here," Richard told Clare on the day she set out from Alameda to drive the boys in her mini-van to Los Angeles.

"After you come over the Grapevine, take The 405 to The 101 West."

"101 West." She wrote it down.

"Wait a minute. It might say 'South,' but it's 'West.' You won't have any trouble."

Even over the phone, she could imagine his gesture: a wave of the hand, an easy assurance.

As it turned out, it wasn't difficult to find Richard's office building—"the tallest and glitziest on Ventura Boulevard," he had said. Richard and Marty had offices on opposite corners of their twelfth-floor suite, both with sweeping views of mountains, the San Fernando Valley and the rivers of freeway. The real rivers of Los Angeles—the ones with water—were encased in concrete and often ran dry.

Clare considered parking in the slot marked "Stone," a prime location close to the garage lobby, but didn't, half-believing that if she left it vacant, Richard would return. It was childish. Superstitious. Step on a crack, break your mother's back. But at some point Richard could return and why not now, when she was upstairs meeting with Marty?

At the lobby's double glass doors she stopped to tuck the parking ticket into her purse, so she didn't see it coming. Afterwards, she was glad her head was lowered so the force of the blow didn't break her nose. She sensed rather than saw someone shove the heavy glass door, felt the impact before the pain came, and then the blood. She wasn't angry right away, just surprised. She called out to the retreating figure in a track suit, an unshaven, thick-necked body-builder type so muscular he walked with his arms bowed out at the elbows.

"Hey! You hit me with the door!"

But the man in the black nylon tracksuit was already getting into his black van. He didn't even bother to look back; he was oblivious to the pain he had caused.

~⊘

Behind oversized wood-framed glass doors in a pleasant, bright space bridging Richard's and Marty's offices sat Diana and Sylvia, their administrative assistants. When Clare entered holding a tissue to her forehead, they hurried around their desks to help her.

While Diana led Clare to one of the deep couches and proffered more Kleenex, Sylvia disappeared down the hall. Clare explored her hairline, from which blood was oozing, then pressed a fresh tissues against it until Sylvia, carrying a wet paper towel, interrupted her.

"Here, Honey—let me get this blood off your shirt." Sylvia dabbed at Clare's blouse, causing the blood stains to fade and spread at the same time.

"I hope you don't get a black eye," Diana said. "That happened to me once." She meant to be sympathetic, Clare knew, but the possibility of a shiner hadn't occurred to her until then.

Marty bustled out of his office, looking harried.

"Whoa! What happened to you?"

Clare explained about the Neanderthal and the glass door while Marty walked her back to his office. He gestured for her to sit in one of two chairs in front of his desk and he sank into the other. Clare touched her forehead with her fingertips. The bleeding seemed to have stopped.

"You're sure you're okay?"

"Yes, I'm fine."

"So what did you want to see me about?"

Marty leaned towards her as she fumbled in her purse for the picture. When she held it out to him, he looked stunned.

"That's Sara Bachrach," Marty said. "Where did you get this?"

"It was in Richard's desk, hidden." That really galled her. That he had gone to trouble to conceal it from her—something she never imagined Richard would do.

She handed Marty the note. "This was with it."

"This note could mean anything. But there's gotta be an explanation." He shook his head. "This is so strange—Sara, the note, hiding the picture." He leapt out of his chair, slamming his hands on its arms. "C'mon. We're going to take a little drive."

Marty maneuvered his Mercedes skillfully, weaving in and out of lanes on The 101, heading east towards Pasadena. Like most of the other drivers speeding along at 80 miles per hour, he was talking on his cell phone, which was clamped firmly between his ear and his left shoulder. The man's voice on Marty's cell phone was loud—louder than Marty's—and angry. Clare looked out the passenger window and tried not to think about what would happen if Marty lost his concentration for even a second. Eventually he grunted, pressed "End" and turned to her.

"Sorry." He laughed. "That guy hung up on me."

"Does that happen often?"

"Naw." Marty floored it to pass a truck, causing Clare's head to snap back. "He's pissed off we won't talk to him. One of our clients, Maya Eastman, was separated from this guy and she just filed for divorce. He's an ex-prize fighter, beats her up. You know Richard's been the firm's spokesman." Clare nodded. Richard had been very excited about his television appearances, recording every one so he could watch them over and over.

"There was lots of publicity when he showed up on the set, threatening everybody in sight. You ever watch the soaps?" He turned his head to look at Clare, who took up the task of watching the road, hoping Marty would get the message.

"She's in *Days of Eternal Love*," Marty said.

"I know that one."

One of her indulgences in Alameda had been a weekly trip to the nails salon, an establishment run by women who spoke little English and murmured back and forth to each other as they bent over their clients' hands. To entertain the customers, an overhead television was kept tuned to the midday soap operas. They weren't hard to follow, even watching only once a week, and she looked forward to the twists in the convoluted plots.

"What does Maya Eastman look like?"

Marty frowned, concentrating. "Short, too skinny for my taste, big hooters. Fake, of course." He glanced quickly at Clare. "Sorry. But you know how it is in LA. Lots of women have them."

"She has blond hair? Shoulder length?"

"Yeah, that's Maya."

"I think last time I watched, Maya was pregnant by her sister's husband, and the sister was trying to hire a hit man to kill her."

Marty winced. "That's too close to reality for comfort. Her life's a soap opera. We've got her at a safe house and there's tight security on the set. Everybody's afraid of Barone and what he might do. If she can get through this divorce without his beating the crap out of her, we'll all be happy." He shook his head. "Barry Barone—what a piece of work."

As Clare took in the San Gabriel Mountains looming stark and majestic above Pasadena, she wasn't really listening to what Marty was saying.

CHAPTER EIGHT

CLARE HADN'T EXPECTED PASADENA TO BE SO BEAUTIFUL, SO DIFFERENT FROM the bare, bleached streets of Agave. She was even less prepared for the long driveway through what seemed to be acres of grounds leading to a shingled craftsman-style house, almost Japanese in appearance, with a covered terrace on one side and a deep porch spanning the front.

A dark-haired woman stood, trowel in hand, dwarfed by glossy *Fatsia japonica* in a shady bed on the house's north side. She turned at the sound of Marty's car, and Clare saw that she was the woman in the picture, smaller than Clare expected, and sharper-featured. She wore a man's blue dress shirt that reached to her knees, baggy jeans and an oversized sun hat. The woman picked her way out of the fern-studded shadows, moving toward them through a bed of white perennials.

"Marty!" she smiled, leaning down into his window and then nodding in friendly way past him to Clare. "This is a surprise."

"Hello, Sara." Marty swung out of his seat with a grunt and stepped around the front of the car to open Clare's door.

"Is everything all right?"

"No," he said, "it isn't. We're here about Richard. We thought maybe you could help us."

"Richard Stone?" The woman looked from Marty to Clare. "Sorry." Marty grasped Clare's arm as if she were an invalid. "This is Clare Stone, Richard's wife."

"I'm Sara Bachrach," the woman said, pulling off one garden glove and extending a small, slim hand.

"I know," Clare said, ignoring Sara's gesture. "I found your picture and note to my husband in his desk."

Sara Bachrach frowned. "Let's go inside out of the heat."

Sara led them up the stone walk and into the cool interior of her house, a wood-paneled, oriental-carpeted nest so lovely and welcoming that Clare forgot for a moment what had brought her here. It was an Arts and Crafts 'bungalow.' Clare had never seen such a beautiful one. In the living room, Sara motioned for her to take a seat on one end of the sofa while she sat at the other. Marty settled himself into one of two wood-and-leather chairs— original Stickleys, Clare thought, or good reproductions.

"Sara," Marty said, leaning forward and clasping his hands, "since Richard's disappearance we've been trying to locate people who might know where he would have gone. After Clare found the picture and note, we came to you."

"Richard Stone? He's disappeared?" Sara sank back against the cushions. "I didn't know," she said, looking from Marty to Clare. "I can't believe it."

"It's been in all the papers," Marty pointed out.

She shook her head. "I just got back from visiting my brother. I haven't kept up with the LA news." Sara reached over and put her hand on Clare's. "I'm so sorry," she said. "What's this about a picture?"

When Clare pulled the photo out of her jacket pocket, Sara studied it, turned it over and then placed it on the sofa between them. She remembered the conference, she said. They had gone together: Richard, Sara, Diana and some others from the office. Diana had taken the picture. Sara had never seen it before, had never given it to Richard.

She dismissed the note written to Richard with a shake of her head. "It's a thank-you note," she said, refolding it and handing it back to Clare. Her husband had been terminally ill and their finances were in disarray. She was afraid she would lose everything. She knew nothing about the "money side of things," she said. Richard had been very helpful, sorting everything out for her, directing other attorneys who rewrote their wills and trust documents so that she would be financially secure.

"Your husband helped me in a time of great need," Sara said. "He has been a good friend." She looked down. "As far as anything more ... that's the furthest thing from my mind."

Clare could hear the fabric of Marty's suit fighting with the upholstery as he squirmed in his chair. Sara must have, too, for suddenly she looked up, her face flushed.

"I can see why"—she gestured towards Clare—"Richard's wife would misunderstand, but you, Marty ... you of all people. You've known me—known Quentin and me—my whole adult life. What on earth were you thinking?"

Marty held out his hands towards Sara, splayed as if to ward off a blow. "Hey!" he protested. "No, no, no! I was just trying to help Clare. She found the picture and it was weird, the way Richard hid it. It's so strange. I thought you could reassure her."

Sara snorted. "I don't see how bringing Richard's wife here could possibly help. I have no idea how or why Richard had this picture or why he hid it. I don't appreciate how you went about this, Marty. Not one bit." She rose from the couch and turned to Clare. "I'm sorry for your trouble, Mrs. Stone, but I can't help you."

Marty hustled Clare out to his car, not stopping to open her door this time. "Goddamn," he said, pulling out of the driveway and onto the main road, "I didn't think this out. Sara wouldn't be involved in any funny business and how could she possibly help? I messed up—dragged you out here for nothing and hurt her besides." He banged his palm against the steering wheel. "Goddamn."

Marty pulled the car onto a side street and stopped. His seat hummed backwards, giving him room to turn sideways and face Clare. She couldn't help noticing how chubby Marty's thighs were. Even with the seat pushed back, he looked uncomfortable.

"You okay, kid?"

Clare shook her head, "No, I'm not okay, but I don't think that woman is having an affair with my husband."

"I don't either."

"I didn't want to believe her, but I do." She glanced at her watch and realized the boys would be at the house before she could possibly get there. She reached over and patted Marty's hand. "And now I need to get home."

~⌒

Marty gunned the engine as he pulled his car onto The 134, heading west towards Encino. The traffic slowed as they approached a freeway interchange. He drummed his fingers on the steering wheel.

"Did Richard seem any different to you lately?"

"No."

She didn't want to tell Marty about the weekend—the sex, the midnight phone call. They drove in silence for a while, the only sound the honking of a car two lanes to their left.

"Do you think he was depressed or something?"

Marty shook his head. "No. Certainly not depressed. Cheerful, in fact, like he was really on top of his game."

Did they all talk in sports metaphors? Clare wondered.

Marty swerved to avoid a car in front of them. At the partners' meeting on Friday, Richard had left them in awe with the scope of his vision. His insights into cases, his business plans for the practice radiated intelligence and, above all, energy. Phil had even protested, not entirely in jest, "Hey, slow down! We can't keep up with you!"

"I don't know much about this psychological stuff, you know," Marty said, "but I think if he were going to harm himself ..." He stopped for a moment, swallowing. "Not that I think that's it, Clare, but if he were, I think he would have acted upset, not so happy, like he was last week."

Clare wondered if Richard had made a mistake he couldn't fix and had fled to avoid facing the consequences. No. He wasn't one to run from a mistake. Besides, he loved it here. He was so enthusiastic about life in Los Angeles, their pool, the view of dry hills.

As if he had read her thoughts, Marty added that he had a message from the accountants that the clients' funds were all intact; there was no evidence that Richard had done anything unethical.

They didn't talk much the rest of the way to the office. Marty pulled into his space, next to the empty spot marked "Stone," and leaned over to kiss her cheek. She could smell his fading aftershave.

"From now on we'll leave the detective work to that guy you hired, okay?" she said.

CHAPTER NINE

WHEN CLARE PULLED UP TO THE HOUSE A HALF-HOUR LATER, SHE WAS SURPRISED to see Jannie in the driveway, standing by a yellow Cadillac convertible next to a swarthy man in a Hawaiian shirt.

"Mom!" Adam ran over to her. "He was ringing our doorbell when we got here. Jannie said she'd wait with me. Matt's in his room."

Jannie waved in greeting, then stepped behind the man so he couldn't see her raised eyebrows. They were an unusual looking pair, Jannie fresh and cool in a sleeveless shift and the odd-looking fellow in too-long chinos, *huaraches* and a straw hat. Clare could hear drivers slow down as they passed the house, gawking. As she approached, the man transferred a chewed unlit cigar to his left hand and held out his right.

"Moe Billingsley," he said. "Marty Berg hired me to help you."

"See you later," Jannie called, climbing into her van. "Good luck!"

"I've got a few questions," Moe said, leading Clare into her own house. He wove his way among the stacks of boxes in the living room and settled onto the sheet-covered couch, grunting as he did so.

"You got an ashtray?"

"We don't smoke."

"*No problema*," Moe shrugged, tucking the wet cigar into his shirt pocket. "You're the *jefe*."

"It means 'boss,' Mom," Adam explained. "It's Spanish."

Matt appeared at the entryway, and Moe gestured for him to join them. Making a wide circle, Matt chose the other end of the couch. "I'd like to ask you all a few questions, help me get some ideas about your father ... and your husband," he added, with a nod to Clare.

"Let's start with this *compadre*," Moe said, beaming at Adam. Clare watched Matt examining Moe in every detail—his sand-colored teeth, the battered hat he had placed on a packing box, and the greasy brown hair, dented all around from the hat's lining. His face was tanned—probably from riding around with that convertible top down—and deeply lined.

"Dad's fun," Adam was saying. "He plays with us a lot—basketball, baseball, soccer. All that stuff."

"Not all the time," Matt cut in. "He's been different lately."

"You'll get your turn, *amigo*," Moe said, nodding his head in Matt's direction. "Let's let this one have his say."

Matt glowered at Clare.

"What did he do if you acted up?" Moe asked.

"Sent me to my room," Adam replied, serious now. "But that didn't happen very often." He looked up at Moe. "Dad's great."

"What about you?" Moe asked, turning to Matt. "How would you describe your father?

"We call Dad 'HyperMan,'" Matt replied, looking at Adam, who laughed.

"You do?" Clare asked.

"Yeah, Mom. You know that."

"No."

"Well, we do," Matt said, turning back to Moe. "He did more than all the dads in the neighborhood. He used to play baseball with us and he was my soccer coach and he's a runner and a cyclist. Saturday he told me he's going to ride in the Tour de France next summer."

"He was kidding you, honey," Clare said.

"He wasn't," Matt protested. "He was serious."

"Okay," Moe sighed. "Has your dad done anything special with you since you've been here?"

"Only once," Matt said. "He took us for a drive one day when Mom was taking a nap. He said it was special. We didn't want to go."

"Oh yeah," Adam said softly. "The banana place."

"What's that?" Moe looked from Matt to Adam and back again.

"Somewhere near the ocean—a place where they sold bananas," Matt said. "Dad knows I like bananas, so he took us there. He really gave it a big build-up, but it was nothing."

"Remember the name?"

Matt shook his head. "No."

"You said it was on the ocean. How long did it take to get there?"

Matt shrugged. "I don't know. Maybe an hour."

Moe turned to Clare. "You agree? Has your husband been different?"

Clare looked down at her lap. "We've all had a hard year. He was living down here while we were up North, trying to sell the house." It was more than hard; it was terrible.

"We didn't see him very often—just on weekends—and when we did, he was very tired."

It took Richard at least three hours to get to the Burbank airport, fly to Oakland, and drive home. When he finally arrived at the door, he'd be exhausted. What little time they had together he spent slumped in his chair, dozing or watching television.

"How about moods?"

"He loves it here ... the constant sun."

"Is your husband a drinker?" Moe asked.

"Not really. A social drinker, I guess."

"Has he been drinking more lately?"

"No. No. There was no change," Clare said.

"Mom, come on!" Matt said. "Sure he has."

Clare looked at Moe. "I haven't noticed that—if he's drinking more." Richard had always liked to drink.

"What about money? Is he careful? Or a big spender?"

"He loves to spend money," Matt said, and Adam agreed. "Oh, yeah." Adam's face lit up. "On Saturdays, he could spend $700 at Costco in an hour!"

"That got a rise out of them," Moe observed. "What about you, Mrs. Stone? Would you say your husband is a big spender?"

"Sometimes." She lowered her head.

"You'll have to tell me what you're thinking. I'm not a mind reader, Mrs. Stone," Moe said, sitting back against the couch. He smiled, as if at a private joke. "Though I try to be." He spread his arms along the back of the sofa so that his Hawaiian shirt pulled at the buttons and Clare could see his pale, hairy belly in the gaps.

"Just that Richard was"—she searched for the right description—"uneven about how he spent money. Sometimes he spent a lot. Sometimes he watched every penny."

"Got a recent picture?"

"Sure!" Adam jumped up and ran to the boxes of photo albums. Those, at least, had been kept up to date until they moved. He came back with the formal photo the firm had taken of Richard—smiling, relaxed, stylish in a summer suit.

"Oh, he's a handsome guy, your father," Moe said. "I can see where you guys got your good looks." He glanced at Clare. "I didn't mean that the way it came out. You're a pretty woman." Moe tucked the picture into his pocket, careful not to disturb his cigar. "Okay, just a few names and numbers and I'm outta here."

He rose and pulled a business card, bent and warm, from the pocket at the back of his pants. Clare held it gingerly by its edge.

"Moe Billingsley," it read, the name framed by two arching palm trees. "Finder of Lost Persons." The address was a post office box in Hollywood. Clare stared at the card.

"What's the matter?" Moe asked. "You find a typo?"

"No." She raised her eyes. "I was thinking what a strange title you've given yourself."

Adam pushed up against her, reaching for the card. "Let me see, Mom." He looked at the card. "Hey! Do you really live in Hollywood?"

"I do," Moe answered, smiling down at the boy.

"By that sign in the hills?"

"Close."

"That's so cool," Adam said.

Moe turned to Clare. "Yeah, well," he inclined his head. "I have different cards with different titles."

"What I meant was, why not 'missing persons'? Why 'lost'?"

"Because they're usually more than 'missing.'" he replied.

Clare shook her head.

"*Amiga.*" He laid his hand on her arm. "I'm saying, one way or another, most people aren't just missing. They're lost."

Through the windows, Steve Rosado watched Clare moving across the kitchen, fixing a meal for her sons. She wasn't pretty in the traditional sense, her features were too strong and she wasn't skinny like most of the women around here—she was curvy, like a woman should be. With her height and coloring, the way she held herself, how healthy she looked—all together, she was beautiful, more beautiful than any of the starlet wannabes you see everywhere in LA.

What was Stone really like, he wondered. He seemed friendly enough, likeable, probably attractive to women. An affair was one thing, but what kind of man would take off and leave his family without even a note? Stone was a fool, leaving a woman like that. You could see she was looking for another reason for his disappearance, not wanting to believe the obvious. Stone could have had an accident, but really, the chances were much greater that he had a woman somewhere. Steve was sure the guy wasn't coming back. And Clare would realize it sooner or later.

Steve continued measuring, setting out stakes and lines. The adobe was hard and dry, and he was having a difficult time driving the stakes into the ground. He wanted to talk to Clare about the garden again, to watch her face light from within as she discovered what she wanted. He was sure any landscape they worked on together would be beautiful. She would need that—something lovely to focus on instead of this ugliness her husband had laid on her.

The wind that usually blew over the hills at this time of the evening shifted, and he could feel the first spatters of rain coming from the west, against his back. He propped his tools inside the garage corner that had been cleared for him, glancing at Clare once more before he left.

Clare heard the gate slam behind Steve Rosado and checked her watch. Five o'clock—not too early for a glass of wine. If she'd thought of it, she would have offered Steve a glass, but maybe he had to get home to his wife. If he had one. He didn't wear a wedding ring, but many men didn't. She swiped crumbs from the boys' snack off the table with her free hand and wondered what sex would be like with another man. Richard was the only lover she had ever had. The first and last, she always believed. Now she wasn't sure.

The wine glass was empty. Another glass this early wouldn't hurt if she could force herself to eat something with it. She found some crackers in the cupboard and washed them down with a second glass of Chardonnay.

Merlin was sitting by the French doors. She opened them and, after a slight hesitation, he strolled in and sat, staring up at her. Treat time. She rustled around for the kitty bits and stooped to feed him, holding out her palm to him. She loved the tickle of his scratchy tongue. When he had finished, she tried to pick him up.

"Stay with me awhile," she coaxed, but the cat wrested himself away, tail twitching, ears flattened. "Do you want to go back out?" she asked, opening the glass door. The rain was coming down steadily now, and Merlin refused to leave. Instead, he slipped past Clare and disappeared upstairs.

~⌒

Clare lay in their bed, staring at the ceiling. The clock read 2:18 a.m. It was strange to hear rain in September—out of place. The rain shouldn't start until November at the earliest. Was Richard safe and dry somewhere, she wondered? Or was this rain falling on him? She was so afraid, and it was so hard to place her trust in the police and Moe. She took a deep breath, then counted to ten. Dwelling on her fears wouldn't help. If she was ever going to get to sleep, she needed to focus on something else, something pleasant like the garden. She plumped up her pillow and turned away from the empty side of the bed. Think about the kind of garden Richard would love, she told herself, though she couldn't imagine what that would be.

Forty miles east in Pasadena, Sara chose Quentin's blue pajamas from the dresser. They were made of cotton so tightly woven they felt silky against her body. She had bought them for him as a small way to ease some of the pain he felt in his last weeks. They would be comforting to wear on a night like this, a night of strange weather, an unseasonable storm. She opened all the windows to let in the sound and smell of the rain. Slithering into bed, Sara rubbed her face into Quentin's pillow and wondered how much longer it would hold his scent.

It had been an unsettling day. Richard Stone missing, Marty on her doorstep with that sad woman. Richard Stone's wife hadn't had anything bad happen to her before, you could tell. She had a confused manner, as if it were all a mistake, as if tragedies happened only to other people. We know better, don't we, she thought, adjusting Quentin's pillow, stuffing it into the hollow of her neck. We know that life can change in an hour, a moment of uncertainty can become a seizure, a diagnosis, then a death sentence. It would take a while for Clare Stone to learn that no one is immune to tragedy.

Sara inhaled deeply. The rain was coming down heavily now, draping the windows with water. When had she last seen Richard? Wednesday. A week ago. She had dropped by his office to sign some papers and they wound up going to lunch. There was something about Richard, not just that he was good-looking but also that he drew people to him. He dominated any room he was in. That day, diners in the restaurant turned to look at them as they passed: Richard, tall, graceful, strikingly handsome with his reddish brown hair and easy smile, guiding her with his hand on the small of her back. She was aware then that she felt a little bit happy. Over lunch, Richard joked about his work and talked a lot. He was enthusiastic; it was one of his charms. Only he hadn't inquired into her life, as he usually did. Richard, unlike many men she knew, listened as much as he talked. But not that day. Last Wednesday he had interrupted her when she mentioned her upcoming trip, talked right over her about his plans for the firm when he became the managing partner. And they were grand plans, far-reaching. Perhaps a bit too grand.

Sara lay back on the pillows, thinking of Quentin. She wished she could talk to him and ask him what to do. She hugged her arms across her chest, rubbing them for warmth and comfort. She wondered if she was the only one of Richard's friends who had noticed he was a little off kilter last week. She didn't really want to talk to that woman again, but she knew Quentin would say she owed it to Richard. You've done harder things than this, he would have reminded her. So it was settled. Tomorrow she would go to wherever Richard Stone's family lived and talk to his wife.

Thank you, Quentin, she said into the dark. Now she could sleep.

CHAPTER TEN

When Clare and Adam arrived at Willow Elementary on Thursday for the first day of school, it was clear the word had spread that it was her husband, Adam's father, who had disappeared. Women stood in small groups, stealing glances in their direction.

She took Adam's hand and waited for the welcoming ceremony to begin. An assortment of adults gathered in clusters on the already-steaming asphalt or waited alone on the edge of the crowd. She assumed they were parents: it was difficult to tell from the way they dressed—short, tight skirts or cutoffs, men in mirrored sunglasses with pony tails—if they actually were parents or older brothers and sisters.

The principal, a woman she had not yet met, strode across the yard towards Clare and Adam, reaching out to shake Clare's hand.

"Mrs. Stone—Charlotte Lawton. I want you to know how much all of us in the Willow community are pulling for you, and we hope your husband is … returns soon."

"Thank you," Clare answered, aware of the parents nearby, listening. She tried to think of something to add, something befitting the wife of a missing man, but her imagination failed her. Maybe that was for the best. Maybe they would mistake her silence for strength.

~~~

At ten o'clock, Clare was on the phone, waiting to talk to Captain McVay, when the doorbell rang.

"I'm sorry to just show up like this," Sara Bachrach said, "but I thought of something that might be helpful to you." Clare flushed, thinking of the scene in Sara's living room yesterday.

"Sure." She clicked off the phone and stepped back, watching Sara take in at a glance the incongruous grandeur of the foyer, with its sweeping curved staircase and oversized chandelier. The house had been a compromise. It was in a good school district and was a relatively short commute to Richard's office, but it didn't feel right to either of them. It had been a practical decision, not a heartfelt one. The rooms were enormous, with pretentious high ceilings, oversized light fixtures and parquet floors coated with a plasticized finish that produced an unnatural gloss—a builder's dream of elegance but not theirs.

"After you and Marty left, I kept thinking about Richard," Sara told her. "Maybe I can help you."

"You might as well come into the kitchen."

Clare pawed through drawers looking for the coffee scoop and filters, pulling first one drawer out, then another and another. When she looked up, Sara was standing at the kitchen table by the pad of notes and doodles Steve had given her at the end of his first day of work.

"Do you mind if I take a look at these?" she asked. "It seems to be quite a project." She waved her hand in the direction of the yard, where the lawn was partially gridded with Steve's stakes and lines.

"Go ahead."

Sara sat at the table and waited to speak until Clare was seated across from her. "I'm sorry I was rude to you yesterday," she said. "I was so angry, especially at Marty." She leaned across the table and put her hand on Clare's. "But please believe me when I tell you that there was nothing between

Richard and me. We were friends. That's all."

"But why would he hide that note?"

"I don't know," Sara replied. "It doesn't make any sense to me, either. But let me tell you what I remembered last night." Sara placed her hands in her lap, adjusted her shoulders, and drew herself together with a tidy, cat-like gesture so striking that Clare half expected to see a tail wrap neatly around her feet.

"I thought Richard seemed a little hyper last week."

It was the second time in two days she had heard that word.

"Last Wednesday when I saw him, he seemed a more extreme version of himself—overly enthusiastic, more talkative."

Wednesday. Clare couldn't remember how he acted on Wednesday. Thursday night he worked late. Friday night he went out with Marty after the partners' meeting. He was a little drunk when he came home. "Maybe Richard has been ... different. But there's been so much going on, so many reasons." She gestured at the unpacked boxes, the barren kitchen, the mess of a yard, all the outward signs of the dislocation of their lives. "What are you getting at?"

"I think the changes in Richard's behavior are important in some way. They could be the key to why he disappeared."

The orgasmic groan of the coffeemaker echoed through the kitchen, which had nothing on the walls, no curtains at the window, to absorb the noise. Clare pushed away from the table.

"I see Steve Rosado is your landscape architect," Sara said, resuming her perusal of the landscape papers while Clare busied herself at the counter.

"You know him?"

"He's a friend. I'm a landscape architect by training. Steve and I went to school together."

So this is the client Richard called for a referral. That explains the perfect garden, Clare thought. The woman has everything—looks, brains, talent, a beautiful house. She's alone, a widow—that was very sad—but at least she doesn't have to worry about money; she said herself that Richard had seen to that.

"What is your training?" Sara asked.

"Graphic arts."

"That's so interesting."

Clare shrugged. For her, graphic design had been a pleasant interlude between high school and motherhood. She chose it as her major at Berkeley because she liked the hours of working in solitude and the modern, airy building where her classes were held. And it was something she was good at: she had been one of the "stars" of the department, winning a statewide competition for design of the university's catalog cover.

"Graphic art—to me it's like landscape architecture," Sara explained. "Except that instead of working with soil and plants, you work with paper and inks. It's all design."

Clare looked away in hopes of warding off further conversation about her so-called career. Still, she hadn't thought of her work in the garden as an extension of her art.

"Did you know that Gertrude Jekyll was a painter before she became a garden designer?" Sara prattled on. "Her eyesight was failing, so she began to use the landscape for her canvas, flowers as her palette."

Clare set two mismatched mugs on the table. She was incapable of holding up her end of this conversation. She was no match for Sara and her degree in landscape architecture. The door chimes came as a welcome interruption, but still Clare started at the unexpected sight of Moe, resplendent in an orchid-and-yellow-patterned Hawaiian shirt, finishing off his cigar.

"Jesus!" Moe squinted at her through the smoke. "What's wrong with you?"

"Sorry."

"Settle down," Moe said. "I got some news. I found the banana plantation your kids were talking about." He bowed his head, suppressing a smile.

"You mean the one in La Conchita?" Sara asked from behind Clare's shoulder.

Moe looked stricken. "*Ay caramba!*"

"You know about it?" Clare asked Sara.

"I own a house there," Sara said. "Richard's been helping me straighten out the legal issues with it." She put her hand to her mouth. "You don't think he could be there, do you?"

They made Moe put the top up on the car, then sped west and north on The 101 towards La Conchita. Clare sat in front, and Sara cleared a place for herself amidst an accumulation of newspapers and crumpled fast food bags on the back seat.

"So what's your connection again?" Moe asked, craning his neck back towards Sara.

"Quentin and I own—well, it's mine now—a piece of land and an old house up there. It's one of the properties Richard put into our family trust. Please keep your eyes on the road," Sara said, and when Moe had, to Clare's surprise, obeyed, Sara continued. "Before my husband's death Richard helped us with some litigation connected to our estate."

"Huh," Moe said. "An estate."

Clare looked back at Sara, who rolled her eyes, then continued: "Quentin's—my husband's—family has owned a house and several lots in La Conchita since the 1920s. They used to spend their summer vacations there, going to the beach. After we got married, I went along, too, and grew to love it. La Conchita has always had such an interesting mix of people—artists, teachers, hippies, small businessmen. Independent types. It's a great place."

"Coulda fooled me," Moe said. "It looks like a dump now—half the houses boarded up and that mountain coming apart behind them."

"What are you talking about?" Clare asked.

It had happened last spring, Sara told her. There were very heavy rains and Rincon Mountain was saturated, so it began to slide. It wiped out several houses and people had to evacuate.

"Moe, I'm surprised you didn't see it on the news," Sara said.

He grunted. "Can't keep track of goddamn everything."

Forty-five minutes later, they careened off the freeway at the La Conchita exit and, at Sara's direction, drove up the incline to Vista del Rincon, the topmost of the tiny town's streets, hunched at the base of a large mountain. The town looked as if it could be a Mexican village: bougainvillea pouring over stucco walls, red and orange vines running riot, and great hanging trumpets of deadly datura. Looming urgently above it all was Rincon Mountain, the raw, bare soil of its innards exposed by the slide. Below the gash lay a path of destruction: parts of wood-frame houses sticking out of the mud like broken limbs. Dwellings not destroyed outright by the slide were canted crazily and festooned with "WARNING! Geologic Hazard Area" signs, cautioning the curious to stay away. It was to one of these tilted houses that Sara pointed.

"That's it."

Moe pulled the convertible up to the curb, hopped out and pulled a duffel bag out of the car's trunk while Sara ducked under the plastic warning tape and, kneeling by the front step, lifted a large stone beneath a passion flower so vigorous it partially blocked the doorway. She looked up at Clare and Moe, squinting into the afternoon sun.

"The key's gone," she said.

"Somebody knew where you kept it," Moe said. He handed his duffel bag to Clare and stepped back. "Here goes!" Moe said, taking a run at the door. It gave way easily to the force of his shoulder and a wall of cold, putrid air pushed back at them.

Clare's stomach lurched. "What's that smell?"

"I think it's in the dirt." Moe gestured towards a pile of rusty-colored mud that had oozed through a break in the cabin's wall.

Sara nodded. "It's anaerobic decomposition. All the stuff that was buried in the slide is breaking down in the mud—decomposing."

Clare shivered. "You all right?" Sara asked, putting an arm around her.

Moe tried the light switch, to no avail. He fished two flashlights out of the duffel and handed one to Clare, then stepped inside, sweeping his own light from side to side until the beam caught a Burger King bag and empty glass on the room's tiny table. Moe rubbed the leftover bits of hamburger bun between his thumb and forefinger and pronounced them "pretty fresh." On the floor beside the armchair lay a nearly empty bottle of vodka.

"Stay here while I make sure things are"—he yanked his head towards the back of the house—"you know." Clare waited, trying to control her breathing.

"All clear," he called, and she flashed the beam down a short passage to a bedroom where Moe stood. The room was clean and bare, crumpled sheets on a double bed but no signs of the sleeper's identity—no clothes, no comb or toothbrush.

"Let's see what else we can find." Sidling past Clare and Sara, Moe illuminated the way to the kitchen. At the door, he jerked to a stop and pointed the beam at splotches on the floor—black, the color of dried blood. "Hold on," he cautioned. "Step back into the hall while I have a look."

Clare could feel the warmth of Sara's body close behind hers and reached back for her hand. Moe had disappeared; there was no sound from him, just the intermittent illumination of his flashlight. Finally, unexpectedly, a chuckle.

"Get a load of this," Moe called. He was standing at the kitchen sink, shining the light on a box of hair dye and a stiffened, dark-stained dish towel. Pools and spatters of the dried black dye stained the countertop and floor. He handed the light to Clare and pulled a trash container out from under the sink, extracting a bag from SavOn Pharmacy in Ventura. The beam wavered in Clare's shaking hand while Moe fished from the bag's depths a receipt for the purchase of Cheez-Its and Clairol. The charge slip was dated Tuesday, September 26, 1995, and signed "R. Stone."

CHAPTER ELEVEN

Moe raced back to Agave, arriving just in time for Clare to pick up Adam, then Matt, at their schools. She made a mental note to see if Jannie could help her out by letting her join the neighborhood carpool. That would take some of the pressure off her and also might be a way for the boys to make new friends.

That night, a small earthquake shook the house shortly after 1:00 a.m., rattling the dishes in their cupboards and jolting the kitchen table where Clare was writing. She looked up and watched the overhead lamp sway. It was undoubtedly an aftershock of the Northridge quake; they could continue for months, even years. She thought of all the time she had spent worrying about earthquakes, never once imagining that her husband would disappear as if he had fallen into a fissure created by one. But tonight the temblor didn't matter. Nothing mattered except that Richard was alive, at least on Tuesday and probably now.

She flipped the pages of the notebook, reviewing the lists she had drawn up with Moe. The La Conchita house was being watched around the clock by Moe's "*compadres*," as he called them, and Clare left a message for Captain

McVay, telling him about their discovery. She wouldn't hear from him until morning, but she was sure the new information would move Richard's case from the "wait and see" file to an active investigation. Tomorrow while the boys were at school she planned to spend time with Moe in Ventura and the coastal towns near La Conchita, taking Richard's picture around to the drug stores and local gas stations to find out if anyone had seen him since Tuesday. Later she would take the boys to Marty's for dinner. Moe was coming, too, and they would compare notes with Marty and Sara, who were calling their friends and business associates to see if Richard had been in contact with any of them.

⁓◯

"Come in, come in," Marty said with an exaggerated bow. "It's good to see you guys," he added, reaching for Matt's shoulder. Matt took a small step back, then shook Marty's hand. Adam wrapped his arms around Marty's waist.

"Hey, it's the big fella," Marty said, returning Adam's embrace, then smoothing the boy's hair with one hand. Marty watched Clare's sons head into the house. "The media room's down the hall on the left," he called after them.

"I always wanted kids," he told her, "but it never happened." He cleared his throat and looked away. "Good idea, kiddo, getting us all together like this. I'm sure we'll find him."

"Thank you for getting the food," Clare said.

"You know Richard would do the same for me. He's my best friend." Clare wondered how many people considered Richard their best friend. She had, certainly, until he disappeared and now she wondered if she had known him at all. The doorbell interrupted her thoughts. It rang a second time, then Sara's voice called, "Hello? Anybody home?"

Sara sauntered in wearing black leggings and a man's amethyst sport shirt, so big it hung to her knees. "It's Quentin's," she said, preempting any questions. "I like to wear his clothes."

"Moe called and said he was running late and to eat without him," Marty

68

said, leading the women to the terrace, where a table was set with cloth napkins and wine glasses.

"You did all this?" Sara poked Marty in the ribs with her elbow. "I'm impressed."

On a long table covered with a cloth that might have been a bedspread, Marty had arranged an ice bucket and several bottles of wine as well as sodas and bottled waters. A platter held a collection of crackers with tiny pieces of cheese on each one, topped by a bit of something—Clare couldn't tell what. There were so many bowls of dill pickles, plates of herring, and platters of crackers and rounds of rye, it looked like Marty was opening a deli.

"You've gone to so much trouble," Clare observed. The thought of eating was repellent.

"And this isn't even dinner," Marty said proudly. "That's being delivered."

The dinner—Thai food from Marty's favorite restaurant on Ventura Boulevard—proved to be delicious. Matt and Adam rushed through dinner, anxious to get back to the media room, while the adults waited to be alone to discuss the search for Richard.

"Come on. You gotta see it, Mom," Adam pleaded as he got up from the table. "It's so cool."

"In a while," Clare said. "I need to talk to Marty and Sara right now." She turned back to her friends. "I wonder where Moe is."

The sun was low in the sky and Marty was lighting mosquito-repellent torches when Matt's newly deep voice boomed from somewhere in the house. "Mom! Come here! Fast!" His fear and panic were evident, and Marty upset his chair as he tried to get to the boy.

"What is it?" Clare called as she and Sara hurried behind Marty. The media room was dark except for a screen that took up an entire wall. Matt and Adam were both standing, pointing to it.

"I think it's Dad," Matt said. "Look at that car. Isn't that Dad's Lexus?" It was difficult for Clare to hear him over the clatter of helicopter rotors and the excited narration of the news reporter.

"We have a high speed chase on The 101 North, just south of Santa Barbara," the skycam reporter announced. Clare could see the ocean to the left, a dark-colored car speeding in the middle lane, followed by four police cars with lights flashing.

"Is it Dad? Is it?" Adam asked, bouncing on his toes. "Mom?"

The sun was setting and the freeway was suffused in red-gold light. The image bounced around the screen as the news helicopter hit turbulence coming off the mountain range.

"We have unconfirmed reports that the driver of the black Lexus is a local attorney who has been missing since Monday," the reporter in the studio announced.

"Oh God," Clare said as Sara squeezed her hand.

"Will they shoot him?" Adam asked, his voice reedy with fear.

"No, Honey," Clare replied, putting her arms around Adam and hoping she was right. This was Los Angeles, after all. He was speeding on the highway, ignoring police signals to pull over. But Richard ... Richard was a white middle class attorney. Respectable. He was driving an expensive car. Surely they wouldn't shoot him.

"Again, for our viewers who have just tuned in. We're monitoring a high speed chase on The 101, between Ventura and Santa Barbara. The driver of the Lexus heading north in the number three lane is believed to be a missing Los Angeles attorney."

"It looks like another car," the newscaster intoned, "not a police vehicle, so far as we know, has joined the chase."

Clare leaned forward, squinting at the screen, as Adam crowed,

"Look! It's Moe!"

And there, behind the four police cars, its top down, bright yellow paint glowing in the sunset, was Moe's car with Moe, unmistakable even from the helicopter above, at the wheel, steering with one arm—his left—while he kept his right arm extended casually across the top of the wide front seat.

"I'll call him," Marty said, flipping a cell phone out of his shirt pocket.

It was surreal, Clare thought, to see Marty punch in numbers beside her and then watch Moe, on the huge screen in front of them, lean to his right and pick up a phone on the front seat.

"Hey!" Marty said. "What's going on?" He pushed the speaker button and held the phone between them.

"I found him," Moe said. "I've got a few cops here to help me. We should have him any minute now."

Sara turned to Clare. "Give me your keys. You and Marty need to go to

Richard. I'll take the boys to your house and wait with them."

"We're watching the chase on TV," Marty told Moe.

"No kidding? Those are news copters?" He sounded pleased. "How does the car look?"

PART TWO

CHAPTER TWELVE

Moe was pacing outside the hospital when Clare and Marty arrived.

"*Amiga*," he said, clamping one hammy paw on Clare's shoulder, "brace yourself."

"Is he hurt?"

"No, but it's not pretty."

Clare could hear a man roaring as soon as Marty pushed open the double glass doors to the ER. She trembled as she looked around the cluttered, open room, searching for Richard. Behind partially drawn curtains, the screaming man lay fastened to a bed by straps at the wrists and ankles, tugging at the restraints. He was unshaven and his eyes, underscored by dark half-moon shadows, were wild and darting. His hair was jet black.

"Could that be Richard?" Clare asked Marty.

"I'm not sure."

They approached the bed slowly and only then could see that it was Richard.

"Let me out of here, you asshole," he was shouting at a policeman who stood at the head of the bed. "I'll sue you till you don't have a penny left."

Clare pressed her face into Marty's chest. "Oh my god. He's gone crazy."

The veins along the sides of Richard's head bulged like earthworms. His hands clenched into fists, and he rhythmically jerked his arms, trying to break the restraints.

"You don't know who I am, do you? You'll find out soon enough." The policeman edged to the right, out of Richard's line of vision.

Richard swung his head from side to side and then caught sight of Clare and Marty. His face lit up with a broad grin. "I knew you'd come and get me." He flopped back on the mattress and giggled. "God, I love you guys." He motioned them toward him, flexing his fingers into a curl.

"Get me out of here," Richard whispered to Clare. He didn't notice she was crying. "These people are holding me until the FBI arrives."

"The FBI?" Clare wiped at her face with the palm of her hand.

"They know I know too much."

She looked at him: sweat dripping from his brow, neck tendons straining.

Marty stepped to the foot of the bed. "The FBI isn't coming, buddy."

Richard tossed his head in exasperation. "For Christ's sake, of course they're coming. They've been trailing me for days. Help me get out of here."

"It's okay," Marty said. "No one's going to hurt you."

Richard stilled for a moment, cocking his head like a parrot, then shouted, "You bastards! You're in on it, aren't you? Get out! You're no help! No help at all!"

Marty put a protective arm around Clare's shoulders, angling her away from the sight of Richard. "I think the doctor's here."

"Hello!" The man who appeared at the gap in the bedside curtain appeared to be in his early forties, short and slight. "Roberto Selva, MD," the name tag on his white coat read, "Department of Psychiatry." He had an unusual face: a genetic scramble that left him with a bit of this, a touch of that: a small nose and big ears that gave him an asymmetrical appearance—but he had a kind face and a gentle manner.

"Mrs. Stone? I'm Dr. Selva."

Clare clutched his forearm with both hands and held on as if her life depended on it. "What's happened to him?"

"Just a moment." He patted her hand, then pulled away and turned to Richard. He took one of Richard's tethered hands in both his own.

"You've been through a terrible time."

Richard began to sob. He thrashed against his restraints and tears poured down his cheeks.

"Oh, what have I done?" Richard moaned, twisting his body. "I've ruined everything—my life, my family, my job. I've lost it all."

Dr. Selva shook his head. "No, you haven't. We'll get you through this."

The doctor turned to Clare and tilted his head, indicating they should step away from the bed. When they were out of Richard's earshot, he said, "He's on overload right now—all circuits buzzing. We've given him an injection of Haldol, an anti-psychotic, and Ativan, a tranquilizer. He's already quieted down a good bit."

"This is quieter?"

"Oh, yes." The doctor smiled at her in a friendly way. "Now. Tell me what's been going on. The police said your husband disappeared for several days. Has this happened before?"

"Never."

Clare glanced back at her husband. Richard had closed his eyes but she could tell he was straining to listen. He frowned as she explained that he had disappeared on Monday and she had not known where he was, not known for sure if he was dead or alive, until an hour ago.

"I didn't know what to think," she concluded. "He was so … irritable … all weekend. I thought he might have left because he was mad at me."

"Shut up!" Richard shouted, his face livid, raising his head off the pillow. "I'm sick of hearing about poor little Clare!" He flopped his head back and squeezed his eyes shut.

"I think I might faint," Clare cried, as Dr. Selva grabbed her under both arms and lowered her into a chair. "Put your head between your legs," he told her. "Breathe evenly." Clare did as she was told and felt the doctor place a comforting hand on the back of her neck, much as her father had done when she was a child. The nausea and light-headed sensation passed but she stayed seated. Selva pulled up a chair beside her.

"Feeling better?"

She nodded. She wasn't dizzy anymore, but she couldn't seem to stop the tears.

"You were saying he was irritable before he disappeared. Was he irritable or was he enraged?"

"I guess you could say he was a little bit of everything."

Selva nodded and she felt as if she had passed a test.

"What about sexual activity?"

"What about it?" She was stalling and the doctor knew it.

"Would you say"— he crossed one leg over the other and clasped his hands around his knee—"he was sexual, more sexually active than usual?"

"No," she lied. There was no way she could talk to this stranger, even if he was a doctor, about Richard and sex. It was too embarrassing. And complicated.

"Is there anyone in his family who is manic depressive?"

"Is that what's wrong with him?"

"Quite possibly."

"What does it mean?"

"It's also called bipolar disorder."

Clare had a vision of two polar bears trudging across a bleak expanse of ice. She'd never heard of it.

"It's a mood disorder, and it can be inherited. People who have it suffer mood fluctuations from very high—the manias—to very low—the depressions. The two poles of mood."

"How can you be sure that's what's wrong with him?"

"Experience," Dr. Selva said. "You see enough people in the throes of mania, and after a while you just know. He shrugged. "Some of it is science, some of it is gut feeling. Like any diagnosis. But yes, I think your husband is manic-depressive and this is a manic episode."

"What are you going to do to help him?"

"We'll keep him in the hospital for observation for a couple of days and go from there. You and I will talk about this a lot more later on. Meanwhile, I suggest you get some sleep. You look like you need it."

He rose and led her back to Richard's bedside. Richard opened his eyes and smiled at them. Clare's heart gave a little jerk.

"Listen, Doc, I appreciate your concern," Richard was saying. He sounded reasonable. "But I don't need to be here. I've got people to take care of me." He gestured with his chin. "My wife, you can see how much she cares. And my pal Marty, my law partner." He raised his voice so Marty could hear him.

"You'll let me go back to work, won't you, Marty?"

Marty approached, shaking his head. "Do what the man says," Marty told Richard. "If the doctor says you should stay, stay."

Richard arched his body off the bed, screaming. "Goddammit! I can't trust any of you! My wife! My best friend! You're in cahoots! Cahoots!" Richard must have liked the sound of the word because he yelled it a few more times, his craziness bouncing off the hard gray walls of the ER, until he stopped, exhausted.

"Listen, man," Marty said in a low voice. "My best legal advice to you is to follow the doctor's recommendation. You know the alternative."

Richard was fully attentive now. "What're you talking about?

"Think about what you've done—just tonight. We'd have to get you a criminal attorney. DUI, reckless endangerment, possibly assault on a police officer. As I see it, your alternatives are hospital or jail."

Richard squeezed his eyes shut and turned his head away. His right foot and leg were jiggling.

"Go home and get some sleep," Selva told Clare. I'll call you tomorrow."

Marty put his arm around Clare's shoulders and she leaned against him. She yearned for her children, Merlin, her own bed.

⁓

Moe was still standing by the double glass doors leading to the parking lot. "Here." He thrust two pamphlets at Clare.

"What's this?"

He shook them a little, pushing them closer to her. "Take them," Moe said.

Looking down, Clare read "Manic Depression: FAQs" on the front of one; the other pamphlet was entitled "Bi-Polar Disorder: You're not alone." She wanted to take them and fling them across the room, burn them, banish this new, strange illness from their lives. But she needed to know what she was dealing with, too, so she kept them.

Moe shifted from one foot to the other. "I thought they might come in—you know—handy."

She leaned forward and kissed his leathery cheek. "Thank you."

It was after 2:00 a.m. when Clare and Marty pulled into the driveway in Agave. Sara met them at the door.

"The boys are upstairs," she said. "Adam's sleeping on the other bed in Matt's room; he didn't want to be alone."

Clare went up and sat by Matt's sleeping form a while, pushing back his hair and listening to the steady rhythm of his breathing. His skin was cool and smooth, no longer soft but not yet rough like a man's. There didn't seem to be any point in waking him; he wouldn't remember in the morning, anyway. She left a note by his bedside: "Dad's okay." Adam lay curled like a grub in the other bed, still dressed except for shoes; she pulled the sheet up over his shoulder. As she reached for the doorknob, he startled her by sitting up.

"Is he okay, Mom? Is Dad okay?"

"Yes, Honey. He's safe," she answered.

Adam smiled. "I knew it," he said, sliding back into sleep.

Alone in her bedroom, Clare placed a sample packet of sleeping pills Dr. Selva had given her on the bedside table. She wouldn't need them, she was so tired. The French doors had come unfastened and rain blew into the room, cool and damp. Still more rain in September? Richard in a psychiatric unit? The world had turned upside down. She changed into a pair of Matt's old soccer shorts and a T-shirt and crawled into bed, but sleep didn't come. She was restless, replaying in her mind the scene in the emergency room and her conversation afterward with the psychiatrist. She picked up one of the pamphlets Moe had given her as she left the hospital. It was there in 12-point type—a list of the signs of mania: irritability, rapid speech, inability to sleep, excessive spending, hypersexuality, grandiosity.

It was mania that had caused Richard to disappear. And that mania wasn't the first, only the worst one so far. She wasn't sure the doctor was right then, but now, at 3:00 a.m., half-forgotten incidents tumbled down upon her, crushing her with the mass of their evidence. Richard's spending binges were unquestionable. She never knew what he would bring home. The splurges on electronics were more frequent and more costly in Los Angeles where there were high tech stores everywhere, but he had been doing this for years.

And then there were his enthusiasms, which required still more spending, for Richard wanted only the best in equipment. In the eighties there had been windsurfing, then model trains after the boys were born. Although these diversions were abandoned as he moved on to other interests, Richard was unable to part with the equipment, so one bay of the garage was stacked with packing boxes full of trains while on the wall hung three windsurfing boards and their long masts. He often said he would like to learn to fly a plane—imagine what that would cost. He said he thought it would be thrilling. And cars, oh the cars. When they first met, he was driving an old MG, a "classic." As soon as his solo practice began to make money, he leased a new Porsche, a turbo-something. But before the lease was up, he lost interest in the Porsche and moved on to a BMW, adding past lease payments to the new one. When Clare questioned the wisdom of that, he brushed her away, explaining that he "didn't have time" to wait. The Lexus, his latest luxury, was just "a reward," he said, "for the Titan of Trusts." There were cars for her as well. He surprised Clare with a new Volvo station wagon the day after Matt was born; they needed a safe car for their new baby, he said. Adam's arrival was heralded by a Range Rover that Richard reluctantly agreed to trade for a mini-van four years ago. Lately he had been talking about a Humvee as soon as Matt got his license. And wouldn't she like a bigger van—maybe a Suburban? Or was she ready for a sports car?

Richard's voice, insistent, bounced around in her head. Why hadn't she noticed that something was out of whack? The signs were there, but she missed them. She sat up in bed, trying to catch her breath. She would take a sleeping pill after all. She would take two.

CHAPTER THIRTEEN

"All I wanna do is have some fun ... Fun, fun. Fun fun fun."

Richard bounced one knee to the rhythm of his chant, then the other, then let the cadence move up his torso. He tried to get back to the lyric, tried to hear Sheryl Crow crooning in his ear, but the chant overtook him.

"Fun fun fun." His shoulders were in on it now and his head bobbed, tuning in to the living symphony his body had become. Whatever they had given him, it had taken just enough of the edge off that he was feeling good again. A woman's face appeared at the small window of his room. Chicken wire in the glass. He turned his head in the other direction, towards the outside. That window was curtained in spatters, droplets, crystals, frogs. It was raining.

"All I wanna do ... fun, fun, fun."

He was chanting in time with the torrent now, one with nature, in harmony with the world. Where the rain's tattoo started and his left off he couldn't tell. Which of them came first? His chant or the rain's? Chicken or egg? Who knew? A sudden rush of wind made his heart race. The face at the chicken-wire window was coming for him, syringe in hand. He squeezed his eyes shut.

Richard dreamed of Connecticut and his mother. It was spring. May. The loveliest month. It was raining frogs, she said—though he couldn't see any—and she took him by the hand and led him outside where they stood, faces to the lowering clouds, and let the rain wash over them. They were having a grand time. After a while he wanted to go back inside, he was soaked through, but his mother wouldn't let go of his hand. She led him farther down the grassy slope—because in the dream it was their real yard, the back acreage of the house where his father still lived—to the marshy edge of the pond. His mother raised her face to the sky again, smiling, the raindrops bouncing off her teeth. Richard tried to break free of her, but she held tightly to him and slowly they began to sink into the muck. She didn't seem to realize what was happening, she was so much taller than he. She had sunk only to her waist but Richard was going under. He struggled and struggled, but his wriggling and pulling only caused him to sink faster. He tried to call for help but couldn't scream.

~⚬

When he opened his eyes, a man was standing beside him. He said his name was Roberto Selva. He was a doctor, he told Richard. A psychiatrist. His psychiatrist.

"We met last night," the doctor said. "In the ER."

Richard didn't respond; it seemed safer not to let on too much.

"Do you know where you are?" Dr. Selva asked.

The less you told them, the better. Nothing to hang you with.

"Do you understand my question?"

Richard nodded. He would give him that much.

"You have been through a very hard time."

Richard closed his eyes against the hot tears that sprang, unbidden.

"We have given you some medication to calm you and to get you through these first few days as comfortably as possible. You are safe."

Again, the drizzle of tears Richard didn't have the strength to hold back.

Selva placed his hand on Richard's forearm. "You will get better."

At nine o'clock Saturday morning, Clare woke to feel Merlin beside her, his warm, soft back pressed into the curve of her body. When she stroked him, he purred, and she thought there was no sound more comforting than a cat's purr. She got up, slipped on her robe, and went downstairs, expecting the boys to be installed in front of the television. Instead, she found Sara Bachrach curled on the couch with her hands, prayerlike, tucked under her cheek. She backed out of the family room as quietly as she could, but before she reached the stairs, Sara sat up, rubbing her eyes. She looked like she was about twelve years old, refreshed and ready for a new day.

"Good morning," Sara said. "I stayed here because I thought you might need me. Were you able to sleep?"

"A little."

"You want to try to go back to sleep? Or shall I make you some coffee?"

It was hard to know what she wanted. "I think I'd like to take a walk."

The rain-washed air was clean and sweet, and for the first time in a week she could leave the house without worrying that she was missing Richard's return or a visit from the police. "Do you want company? Sara asked. "Or would you rather be alone?" When Clare hesitated, Sara stood up. "You walk and I'll make coffee so it will be ready when you come back."

"No. Walk with me. I'd like that. It'll just take me a minute to change my clothes."

Clare left Matt and Adam a note promising to bring back cinnamon rolls and they set off for Starbucks taking the long way, down Grey Rock Road to Thousand Oaks Boulevard.

"Wouldn't you think people would have more imagination than to plant these?" Sara asked, pointing to a neighbor's flowerbed. "And all the houses have identical landscapes: berms with day lilies and *Agapanthus*. Pitiful." Clare suppressed a smile. Only a gardener would harbor such strong opinions about plants.

They turned left onto Thousand Oaks Boulevard and the traffic picked up: four lanes full of cars zoomed by, their license plates self-congratulatory: USC GRAD, TOPCPA.

"Los Angeles. The land of vanity plates," Sara said. "No one is really from here, they have no past, so they advertise their credentials on their cars. Instant history."

Clare thought guiltily of Richard's license plates. But Sara was right. No one was from here; Agave Hills was established in 1970. The whole place was brand new, a town with no center, a city made for drivers, laid out twenty-five years ago in a great concrete grid of main streets, bordered by winding roads ending in cul-de-sacs.

Starbucks had arranged tables under an awning on the sidewalk, but the Kanan Road traffic was heavy and the air thick with gas vapors, so Sara and Clare decided to go inside. A couple of women in jogging shorts glanced up as they entered—one even pulled down her sunglasses to get a better look. They knew who Clare was: the Northern California transplant whose husband was missing.

"I think it would be better to sit outside after all," Clare said, returning the woman's gaze.

Sara sipped her café mocha, then smiled at Clare. She seemed completely comfortable, content to sit there with her coffee, feeling no need to say anything.

Clare stirred her cappuccino's foam, flipping it into little peaks. "Marty told me you lost your husband."

Sara nodded. No one ever said "dead." There were always the euphemisms: "lost," "passed away," or—in the shorthand version—"passed." "But he didn't say why."

Why. There was no reason why. "A brain tumor," Sara answered. "A bad one." As if there were such a thing as a "good" brain tumor.

"Is it hard for you to talk about?"

"No," Sara said. It wasn't the talking that bothered her. She had turned the nine months of Quentin's illness over in her mind so many times, viewed it from so many angles, that she had it packaged for presentation—the long or the short version, it didn't matter, she could talk about it to anybody. It was the reality that hurt. She looked up at Clare, still and waiting.

"It started with a seizure. I thought he was having a heart attack," Sara said, "so I called 911. They came quickly, and I followed the ambulance to the hospital in my car. I waited a long time in the ER. I've never been so frightened."

"You didn't want to ask one of your friends to come and sit with you?"

"Friends?" Sara shook her head. "Quentin was my friend; he was the only one I wanted to talk to. The others—they were just neighbors or acquaintances, not anybody I would call in the middle of the night."

When Clare looked puzzled, she continued.

"I think it's more common for childless couples to be wrapped up in each other. We didn't have much in common with people who were raising children, people like you," Sara said, "with busy, complicated lives."

Clare thought of their new house: the still-packed boxes in every room, dirty socks under the couch, the scruffy, sun-burnt garden.

Sara leaned forward. "We had each other. Quentin had his work; I had mine. We were content."

A nurse led Sara to a special room to wait and treated her so gently that Sara knew it had to be bad. When she asked, the nurse said only that the doctor would be in soon to discuss Quentin's "condition" with her. If it's a "condition," then he can't be dead yet, Sara thought. Unless death was considered a condition.

"The neurosurgeon said there wasn't much time, so I told him to go ahead with the surgery. Those days afterwards, waiting to see if he'd wake up, wondering what lay ahead—I can't tell you how awful it was. So lonely."

Sara hadn't talked about the loneliness before. It made people uncomfortable, just hinting at it. But Clare could understand, she knew.

"Looking back, I wonder how I got through it. But people do, because …"

Clare nodded, but she was no longer thinking of Sara. "Because they have to," she said.

～◯

On the doctor's advice, Clare held off visiting the hospital for a few days to give Richard time to "stabilize." Now, walking down the long tiled hall toward his room for the first visit, her pulse quickened at the prospect of seeing him. She hoped he would be the Richard she knew, not the raving madman in the ER.

Richard was sitting in a chair in the corner near the window, the sun streaming across the *Los Angeles Times* spread out across his legs. He was sliding his index finger rapidly back and forth across the columns.

"Hey!" He looked delighted to see Clare standing before him.

"Hi," she said, smiling as she leaned to kiss him. "Reading about the O.J. verdict?" It was all over the news—yesterday's "Not Guilty" verdict sent shockwaves across LA, widening the existing fissure between the black and white *Angelenos*.

Richard looked confused. He clearly hadn't been reading the paper at all.

"It doesn't matter. How are you?" She touched his cheek and lingered a moment, breathing in the familiar scent of his skin.

"Never better!" he beamed.

Clare turned away and reached for the room's second chair, planning to slide it next to his, but Richard had other ideas. Grabbing her hips, he pulled her backwards, onto his knee.

"There!" he grinned.

Clare tried to balance herself, feeling both foolish and pleased.

"So what have you been up to while I've been locked away in here?" Richard asked. He slid his hand up under her sweater and squeezed her breast.

"Don't!" she said.

"What?" His eyes were wide and innocent, but he relaxed his grip.

Clare took a deep breath. "I've been taking care of our boys."

"Oh, that's great. That's great. Tell them 'hi' for me."

Richard moved his hand towards her again, flexing his fingers so that his hand looked like a spider, crawling along the chair arm towards her. She glanced at him to see if he was joking, but he was watching his own hand, fascinated, as it made its way up her arm and over her shoulder.

"Richard," she warned, and he quickly withdrew his hand, gripping the chair once more.

"They really want to see you," she continued as he nuzzled her neck.

"Who?" The hand was under her sweater again, sliding up her back, fumbling at the hooks on her bra.

"The boys. Stop that or I'll leave."

Richard pulled away. "Okay. Okay." He stared out the window, frowning. He looked ridiculous with that black hair. She wondered how long it would take to grow out.

He turned back to her. "Listen, Kittycat. Listen to me." He hadn't called her that for years. She had forgotten the nickname and it pleased her to hear it again. She smiled.

"What's so funny?" he asked. "Here I am in this hellhole, and you think it's a big joke."

"No, that's not true," Clare protested. "I was smiling because you called me 'Kittycat.' " But he wasn't listening.

"Take me home. Get me out of here."

"Richard … I wish I could, but you need to be here for a while."

"No." His eyes were pleading, tear-filled. "I've got things to do. My desk … my cases." He faltered and his voice broke. "The boys."

She reached out and stroked his dreadful hair. He must have taken the gesture as encouragement, for one of his hands was back under her sweater, the other at her waist. "Don't you want me to come home?"

"Of course I do, but you need to stay here for just a little while."

His fingers clawed at her back as he tugged at the bra's hooks, pulling her closer with his other arm. Clare pushed him away. "Don't!" She rose. "I'm going to leave now."

Richard grabbed her arm and pulled her towards him, squeezing one breast so hard that she cried out in pain. "Stupid bitch," he said.

As she hurried down the hall, looking back to make sure he wasn't following her, she could hear him yelling. Two orderlies rushed past her as she turned a corner and fled.

CHAPTER FOURTEEN

CLARE STOOD AT THE BEDROOM WINDOW AND ADJUSTED THE SLATS ON THE SHADE so she could observe the men below without being seen. The crew was still stripping the yard of unwanted vegetation; in a few days they would start amending the soil, adding humus to provide nourishment and aerate it so the plants would thrive. Steve was folding his cell phone and slipping it into his pocket as he walked toward the other men, who were taking a break. What would it be like, she wondered, to have married a man like that—a man with her interests and sensibilities, a man so comfortable in his own skin. And sane. She wondered what he was like in bed, if he was patient and considerate, or if he was in a hurry and demanding.

Steve raised his arms above his head and stretched like a cat, exposing a patch of curly dark hair between his T-shirt and the waistband of his jeans, and Clare felt a flash of heat between her legs. It had been weeks since she and Richard had made love—if making love was what you could call it. She knew now what she hadn't known before—that Richard's periodic hunger for frenzied, frequent sex was a symptom of mania. At those times, as far as he was concerned, she could have been anyone; she was a mere receptacle.

One of the men must have seen her at the window and said something, because Steve turned suddenly, looked up at her and waved. Clare returned his wave, mustering a friendly smile. There was nothing to do but go downstairs and pretend she hadn't been spying on him. She checked her makeup in the mirror by the bedroom door and wished she had time to put on some lipstick.

Steve was waiting outside at the French doors and the men behind him were packing up their tools. His smile was dazzling—those white teeth against his tanned skin. She wondered if he bleached them. Bright white teeth were all the rage in Los Angeles.

"I have a couple of questions," she said.

"Anything."

Clare blushed. "Do you have the landscape plans with you?"

In the few minutes it took for Steve to retrieve the documents from his truck, Clare inspected the staked outline of the pergola. Richard's idea to add it was a good one, even if it was his mania that willed it into existence. In good weather—which was most of the time—it would be a pleasant, shady place to sit and enjoy the garden.

Steve spread the landscaping plans out on the patio table, anchoring the corners with stones. "Look at this." He leaned across her, so near that she detected a faint, not unpleasant smell of sweat. With his right hand he pointed to the lists of plants on the sheet.

"I used all the colors you wanted—purples, yellow, some gray and white—and added a few others. See what you think."

Clare watched his long, tan index finger trace a pattern on the page. He had such beautiful hands.

"Shall we start with the walls?" Steve asked.

The cement block walls that separated the lots of their housing development were prison gray. "I suppose so," Clare said. "I hate them. They're hideous."

Steve laughed. "A woman of strong opinions. I like that."

He riffled through the oversize pages of blueprints until he found his rendering of the proposed wall.

"It looks different," Clare said. "More closed in. Why would we want to do that?"

"Enclosed spaces can be lovely," Steve said. "Los Angeles is full of Spanish courtyards that reminded the settlers of their homeland—spaces open to the sky but private as well. A walled garden is, as we say, 'of the place'—it fits here in LA."

"How will you get us from there"—she gestured at the eight-foot gray concrete fence—"to here?"

"We'll hide the concrete behind a layer of yellow plaster so beautiful, you'll want to be here all the time." He swept one arm in a wide arc, encompassing the whole back yard and reminding Clare briefly, uncomfortably, of Richard. "You'll want to spend all your time in your garden—it will be that seductive."

Clare ducked her head, hiding her face with her hair. "What about the plants?"

"Ah, yes, the plants! The sun bleaches everything out, so we need to use bold colors that can stand up to it: hot, exciting colors—oranges and deep, dark purples."

Clare had always liked pale, cool colors: blue, silver, lavender. But this was Los Angeles, after all, and she wanted a garden that was, as Steve said, "of the place." She could revise her ideas about what a garden should be, break out of old patterns, not plant the same old thing. "Show me," she said.

Steve pulled a book from a stack he'd brought and opened it to pages marked by yellow sticky notes. "Okay. Here's what I suggest." He straightened, squinting in the bright light despite his sunglasses. "Something dramatic—sculptural plants that will play off each other against the soft-colored background of the walls." In front of her he laid out pictures of plants she had seen only in botanical gardens: agaves with foot-long blue-gray leaves, squat palms and statuesque cannas.

"What is this?" She pointed at a tangled, spiked cactus-like creature.

"That's *Aloe arborescens*. It's amazing! I picked it because it will writhe against that wall." He indicated a central point along the back fence and Clare wondered what a bush 'writhing' there would possibly look like. But what did she know? This was Los Angeles, a different climate zone.

"I'd like to soften the look a little," she said. "You seem to have put in a lot of tall vertical plants. What about something shorter and rounded? Do you think sea lavender would work? It looks soft and gentle, even though it's as tough as can be."

In the silence that followed, Clare was sure that Steve thought her taste pedestrian.

"Sea lavender is good," he said at last. "We can add that. And I did include soft, rounded plants; I just hadn't gotten to them yet. Like these echiums. They're upright but not rigid. And bird of paradise—we have to have them. Look at this!" He held up a color photo of a four-foot tall plant: orange and purple with a thick blue-green stalk. In profile, it did look birdlike, as if it had a beak and a topknot of plumage.

"Don't you think it's a bit much?" Clare asked.

"But it's the official flower of Los Angeles," he protested.

Clare flipped through the pages of plant groupings. "Do you have a sketch of the whole garden so I can see what all this looks like together?"

He paged through the pile. "Here's the plan: sculptural forms in combination with softer, rounded shapes to create waves of color. The overall effect is of motion. Nothing frenetic—just slow, undulating movement. The contrast is what makes it so exciting."

"I've never thought of a garden as exciting," Clare mused.

"You will," Steve said, smiling down at her. "Trust me, you will."

CHAPTER FIFTEEN

DR. SELVA ASSURED CLARE THAT RICHARD'S MOOD HAD STABILIZED TO THE POINT where it was necessary to move him, adding that the hospital was only for people who were acutely ill; patients who showed signs of improvement were either sent home or transferred to less medically intensive centers. Richard didn't seem stable to Clare. He was alternately ebullient and tearful. He complained of pain, said he couldn't sleep, begged her to take him home. When she refused, firmly, as Dr. Selva had counseled her to do, Richard threatened to sue her, to sue the doctor, Marty, everybody. Clare found Richard's threats to be the one bit of humor in the whole sorry mess, but as the days wore on and his talk of lawsuits became more insistent, she began to worry.

"Can't you talk to him?" she asked Marty.

"Kid, I tried. I can't get through to him. He's way out there."

Marty feared that if Phil Wentworth knew the entire truth about Richard's illness, he would find a way to ease him out of the firm—some sort of gentlemanly payoff in keeping with Richard's contract of employment, of course. He had the feeling that the label "manic depressive" would put an end to his friend's career. Marty glossed over Richard's sudden disappearance and the freeway chase, though it had been covered in the newspapers, telling Phil that Richard had been under a "strain" and "suffering from exhaustion." For his part, Phil didn't delve into the details and agreed, but grudgingly, that Richard's salary would be continued, provided he returned to work by mid-November.

~

On a golden afternoon in the second week of October, Richard was admitted to a private treatment center near the village of Ojai, south of Santa Barbara and an hour's drive northwest of Agave Hills. Passing through the village, Clare wished she had time to stop at some of the art galleries lining the main street, but with spending time with Richard and then rushing home to pick up the boys at school, it seemed doubtful that she'd have that luxury any time soon. Maybe when Richard was well again—if that time ever came—they could explore Ojai together. It seemed an impossible dream; even if he were to recapture his former self, Ojai would be associated with this dark period of his life, a time they would both want to forget.

Beyond a fringe of palm trees at town's edge, surrounded by orange groves, the Center lay in the shadow of the Topa Topa Mountains. Its architecture, like much of the town's, was in the Spanish revival style: low stucco buildings with tile roofs, open-air arcades and tiled courtyards.

"This place looks like a country club," Clare told Selva, who was waiting for her in the Center's lobby.

He nodded. "If you don't look too closely." When he saw her surprise, Selva added, "All the security measures, locks and so on." He took her arm and walked her to a wall of windows facing the mountains.

"Look. "He pointed at the peaks beyond. Clare drew in a sharp breath.

"I've never seen light like that."

"Yes," Selva agreed. "It's even better at sunset. People around here call the way it glows then 'the pink moment.'"

"I wonder if I could paint that—capture that light," Clare mused.

Selva looked surprised. "I didn't know you painted."

"I used to. I was thinking of starting up again."

"Will you show me your work sometime?"

Clare flushed. "If I manage to come up with something I like."

He smiled. "I think that's very good—to take up something creative at this time."

"So you're my psychiatrist now, too?" Clare laughed. "Really, I think one member of the family is enough."

Selva laid his hand on her arm. "Sorry. It's an occupational hazard."

She was thinking how grateful she was to have someone like Dr. Selva to turn to, when her thoughts were interrupted by the sound of coughing. Clare and the doctor both turned to see Richard, his shoulders hunched like a bird of prey, standing a few feet behind them.

"You two enjoying yourselves?" He turned away before they could answer and walked back towards his room, still talking but now to an unseen listener.

Richard opened the door to Conference Room B. "Class," they called it, Selva said. It was the patients' preferred term for their daily sessions. The doctor prescribed a routine of group therapy with other patients who were emerging from manias or coping with depressions. "The Center has many, many professionals just like you," Selva had told him. Meaning "professionals gone haywire," Richard thought, looking around the room. Attendance at the daily meetings was part of his path to recovery. After "class," there was a period of free time, then lunch, a private session with Selva, then art therapy, dinner, and finally an evening of television in the common room, where thirty patients argued over which program to watch. Usually the dispute was settled by one of the nurses, who invariably chose something unsatisfactory to all.

They watched you carefully here; too many "professionals just like him" had tried to kill themselves, apparently. Razors were prohibited; he couldn't even shave himself. So every morning he had to wait for the nurse's aide— Frank, a big weight lifter with a shaved head—to come around with the electric shaver so that Richard could, in Frank's presence, perform the simple task he had done thoughtlessly for more than thirty years: start the day with a clean shave.

The conference room was as he had imagined: a circle of chairs. He supposed they were going to "share" their feelings for an hour. One wall was taken up by a rectangular mirror—really a window—behind which people could watch the group, unseen. The gray carpet smelled new and the walls were a soothing pale color he couldn't name. He supposed the goal of this subdued palette was serenity. He rubbed his hands together and took a deep breath. It was unusual to be nervous; he used to be confident that he could deal with any situation, but since the "incident," as he thought of it, he felt unsteady, off his game.

Some of the people who were already seated nodded at Richard in greeting; others glanced at him, then looked away. He wondered what they knew. A couple of patients sat with drooping heads, staring at their hands or at the floor. One heavy-set woman gnawed at her fingernails and, when she caught Richard's eye, flashed a wide smile.

A stocky middle-aged man rose from his chair and approached, asking, "Richard?" He nodded and the fellow held out his hand. "Blair Devlin. I'm the facilitator." He indicated an empty chair. "Let's get started, everyone."

It reminded him of his first day of kindergarten. Devlin announced that the class had a new member, told them Richard's first name and occupation and asked that they go around the circle, giving the same information and "sharing whatever was on their minds." There were seven other patients, men and women dressed as neatly as a person could without a belt. Richard tried to remember their names: Sally, Mike, Greg, Enrique, Patricia, Lydia and Bob. Attorneys, a stockbroker, one CPA, a teacher and a vice-president of sales for some company he had never heard of.

Greg, overweight, probably in his early thirties, stated in a flat monotone that he couldn't imagine being on Lithium forever; he couldn't think straight when he was taking it. How would he be able to go back to his job as a stockbroker, he asked, his voice cracking. Others chimed in with stories of their own searches for the perfect dosage or combination of drugs that would return them to normal. Dark-eyed Lydia, so pale she looked as if she hadn't seen the sun in years, commented in a toneless voice that she didn't want to live like this. Greg nodded in agreement.

When his turn came, Richard got a few laughs by recounting how he got here; the freeway chase was a big hit. Beyond story-telling, though, he didn't know what to say. He assumed that an upbeat attitude would get him out of here sooner, so he told them he felt fine—never better.

"Everybody feels fine at first," Enrique said.

"Then you take a dive." Sally took up the story. "What goes up must come down."

"I don't think so," Richard said. "Now that I know what's wrong with me, I'm going to deal with it." He was sure that most of these people were losers—self-pitying and negative. They didn't want to get better.

"He thinks this is easy," Mike said, looking towards the others. "He'll learn."

Richard knew the type—always had to have the last word. He glanced over at Bob, a small man with peaked eyebrows and a merry expression. Bob was chuckling and shaking his head. At least somebody agreed with him.

CHAPTER SIXTEEN

CLARE WAS SCHEDULED TO TALK TO DR. SELVA ONCE A WEEK. SHE WASN'T SURE if this time with him was supposed to be psychotherapy for her or just an exchange of information between them; it seemed to be a bit of both.

"He won't be fully functional for at least a couple of months," Dr. Selva warned Clare at their first meeting. She fingered the edges of a notebook she had brought with her to record what he said

"He thinks he's normal now, but that's the mania. In a matter of days or weeks, he'll become depressed. We can temper the depression with a combination of medications and if we're lucky, it won't be severe."

She wrote what Selva said in an accounting notebook she had picked up at a drug store on the way to Ojai. It was large, imitation black leather with a maroon spine and corners, trimmed with a little embossed golden chain, each gilded oval linking with the next. She planned to use it to track the course of Richard's illness. Everything would be accounted for. No missing pages.

"If he stays on his meds, which is doubtful—bipolar patients rarely keep taking their medications—we should be able to prevent future manias with Lithium and Depakote and in that way avoid the depressions that follow."

"Do depressions always follow?" Clare asked.

The doctor nodded. "Often. But they may not be severe. Time will tell."

"I still have a hard time believing he's bipolar," Clare protested. "He's never missed a day of work."

Selva put down his coffee cup and continued. "Certain legal specialties are very well suited to manic-depressives. A lawyer works very intensively on a particular case, maybe something that's coming to trial. He seems to have boundless energy, needs very little sleep, and does a spectacular job. Then he goes into a decline. Episodes of high energy followed by a let-down occur periodically. They can be linked to the seasons; manias are more common in the summer, depressions in the spring and fall."

The image came to Clare of Richard sitting in his favorite chair, covered with a quilt and sipping hot tea. The very picture of him slumped there made her feel light-headed. It happened every fall. It was a joke between them that as soon as the boys went back to school, Richard would get sick. She hadn't considered that his annual autumn illness could have been a symptom of manic depression.

She looked up to see Dr. Selva watching her. "It's not your fault," he said.

One day after class, Bob caught up with Richard in the hallway and asked if he'd like to join him on his daily walk. It was a spectacular autumn day more common to the Northeast than California. Rain had cleansed the air, leaving the sky a sharp, dark cobalt. The boulder-pocked Santa Ynez Mountains loomed steep and jagged over the narrow Ojai Valley, making Richard uneasy. He mistrusted their abrupt rise. The slightest tremor could send earth, trees and rocks crashing down.

Bob sauntered along the pebbled path winding among the scrub oaks, oblivious to the danger. He talked about the various characters he had met in the three weeks he had already spent here, describing their foibles. It turned out that the freeway chase—which Richard had imagined would make him notorious among the Center's patients—was mild compared to some of the manic crises that had prompted others' hospitalizations. One fellow had been picked up on the Hollywood Freeway at 2:00 a.m., where he was spotted running naked in the southbound center lane, screaming that aliens were after him. Another guy, a senior vice president of an LA-based corporation, had bought new Land Rovers for all ten of his immediate subordinates; after a call from the auto dealership, his wife had persuaded him to admit himself—one more time—voluntarily.

"And what about you? What did you do?" Richard asked.

Bob held both forearms out, then turned them over so his wrists were exposed. Raised red scars extended in two neat lines from below each palm. Richard could see indentations where the stitches had been.

"Jesus!" Richard murmured.

"I hit rock bottom."

Richard sank down on a bench perfectly situated to provide a view of the valley reaching into the purple distance, the sort of placement Clare would have devised. "But you seem so normal," he protested.

Bob grinned. "Well, I'm about ready to be discharged, for one thing. I wasn't so 'normal' when I first got here." He leaned back and shut his eyes, turning his face to the sun. "And I'm not exactly a stranger to manic depression, you could say." He raised his head and looked at Richard. "How're you doing with all this?" indicating the center and its grounds sprawled below them. When Richard didn't answer, he added, "It's hard, especially when you're still pretty manic."

Richard waited. How could Bob tell what was going on with him? Had he let on too much and if so, when?

"Did you ever think the radio commentators and billboards were communicating directly to you?" Bob asked.

Richard shook his head.

"I did. The billboards were the worst," Bob chuckled. "You know how many there are around Los Angeles. Everywhere I turned I saw a billboard that I was sure had a message meant only for me."

"I thought government agents were after me," Richard confessed. "It was crazy."

"It was mania," Bob said.

That night, as he began to drift towards sleep, Richard thought about what Bob had said regarding his mania. He still had a hard time believing there wasn't someone following him. Okay, maybe it wasn't government agents, but these intuitions that had served him so well in his legal career—they didn't come from nowhere, did they?

A memory of his mother flitted through his consciousness, evasive as a bat at dusk. "Be careful," she warned, looming over him.

"Of what?" He didn't understand her fears.

"We're being watched." She pointed to a cartoon cut from one of her magazines and taped to the kitchen wall: "This is the Watchbird watching you." It was a large black bird, mynah-like, peeking around a corner. He thought it was a joke; his mother thought it was real. Maybe it was the McCarthyist paranoia of the time or her imagination running wild. Whatever it was, he remembered how much her warning frightened him.

~⊙

Richard shivered a little and wished he had brought his jacket. The weather had become unpredictable. One day the bright sun bathed the mountains in light; the next a pale, chilly haze obscured its rays. He remembered the unsettled period between summer and fall in New England: frost one day, seventy degrees the next. But in Southern California he was at a loss. He hadn't lived here long enough to know what to expect of the seasons. If there were seasons. Whatever was going on with the weather now, it made him feel anxious. And he was having trouble sorting out if it was the weather that unsettled him or Bob's imminent departure.

"You remember I'm being discharged on Friday," Bob reminded him. "But I'll be at home for a week, and then we'll leave for Cabo San Lucas."

"I wish you weren't leaving." Richard cleared his throat. "Who the hell am I going to hang out with? Maybe when you get back to LA we can get together—for a drink or something."

Bob smiled, squinting into the sun. "It'll have to be 'or something.' Alcohol and Lithium don't mix, remember? But we'll get together. For sure."

"You really do that?"

"Do what?"

"Follow their rules? Don't drink?"

Bob tilted his head in the peculiar, birdlike mannerism he had. "You start messing with your medications, you get into trouble. So I do what they say. I stay away from alcohol and I take my Lithium."

Richard glanced at the furrows on Bob's wrists. Sure. Bob followed the rules until he broke them.

~⦾

On Friday Bob's wife, Linda, a pale-skinned, pale-haired woman, waited by the car while he and Richard said their goodbyes. As Bob turned away, Richard was suddenly afraid he would never see him again. He knew all about the surf at the point where the Pacific Ocean meets the Sea of Cortez; he and Clare had stayed there once when the boys were small. The waves there were gigantic, the undertow fierce. All Bob would have to do was stray just a bit too far on the wet sand, get knocked down and sucked under. A tragic accident, the authorities would conclude, but Richard would know better. He wanted to run after the car, down the long drive, waving his arms to make Bob stop so he could beg him not to kill himself, but his legs felt heavy and he couldn't move. Instead, he stood and watched Bob's car disappear down the road.

CHAPTER SEVENTEEN

CLARE DREADED HER VISITS TO THE CENTER. AS THE DAYS PASSED, RICHARD HAD sunk deeper and deeper into depression. Since his friend Bob left, he would hardly talk to her. Instead, she would sit and hold his hand while he stared, expressionless, at whatever was on the television. Sometimes she turned the TV off, but he continued to stare at it anyway.

The visits with Dr. Selva provided some small comfort. He reassured her that Richard's depression would pass and eventually, as long as he took his medication, he would return to normal. She looked forward to their meetings because Selva was the only person she could talk to honestly about Richard's condition. Even with Sara and Marty, she downplayed the depression's severity so as not to jeopardize Richard's chances for returning to work.

One late October morning, at the beginning of her session, she handed Selva a bill from the Center's laboratory that arrived in the previous day's mail.

"I have a question. I understand the professional fees and the room charges, but what's the lab work for?"

Selva frowned. "The accounts office can help you with that. Any lab work is part of the routine admissions procedure. I don't have anything to do with that."

"Then you can't tell me why he was tested for HIV?"

Selva's face took on the impassive expression that Clare found annoying.

"As I said, there are routine admissions procedures."

"I don't believe you."

"Well," Selva said, resting his clasped hands on the desktop, "I'm telling you the truth."

"Why is an HIV test routine? Do you think the patients are going to engage in homosexual activity while they're here?" Clare asked, flushing in spite of her resolve to stay composed.

"It's unlikely."

"Then why the test?"

Selva cleared his throat. "It's very common for individuals in the throes of mania to be highly sexualized and promiscuous."

"And was Richard?"

"You know I can't tell you that."

"You can."

"No, there is such a thing as doctor-patient confidentiality, you know." He didn't meet her eyes.

"Please, I need your help," Clare pleaded.

After a few seconds, Selva looked up at her, a pained expression on his face. "You're not at risk for HIV."

"How do you know?"

"The test results. We test almost everyone admitted here for HIV."

"Almost everyone? You tested Richard. You suspected something."

Selva's expression softened. "Clare, you know a lot about manic depression now. You know that people are driven by their manias to do all kinds of things that are uncharacteristic and that are, in a sense, out of their control."

Clare looked down at the envelope in her hands and saw that she had nearly twisted it in two. "But did he have sex while he was missing?" She tried to read the answer in Selva's face.

"Whatever he may have done, he had lost the ability to act rationally."

"So he did have sex with other women then."

She could see him hesitate, then look away. His answer, though unspoken, was clear.

Clare stuffed the bill and torn envelope back into her purse with shaking hands. She wanted to leave before she started to cry.

The doctor reached across the desk towards her.

She stood. "I have to get out of here."

She yanked at the heavy door and strode down the hall, not catching Selva's last words. Whatever he said, she was too far away to hear him.

It was twelve o'clock when Clare got home, giving her three hours before the boys would be home from school, three whole hours to compose herself. She poured a glass of wine—it was only noon, but she was entitled after what she'd learned this morning—then went outside and paced back and forth on the patio, moving from sun to shade and back again, then circled the pool.

She reviewed the conversation with Dr. Selva and what she saw as his admission that Richard had had sex with other women. True, Selva was careful to remind her that Richard wasn't in his right mind; it was the mania that drove him. That should have been a solace, but the thought of Richard making love to another woman, giving some other woman the pleasure that belonged to her, was intolerable. She squeezed her eyes shut, trying to erase the mental picture of Richard having sex with someone else. She could see the muscles in his arms tense, feel his skin, his beautiful back, hear him moan as he entered her.

"No!" she cried out loud. She could hardly breathe from the pain she was feeling, and it was no consolation that this was an old story. She thought of how she had reacted to her friends' husbands' affairs with sympathy, all the while safe in the smug belief that this would never happen to her.

On her second circuit around the pool, Merlin appeared, trotting along the blocky fence top. As he neared, his pace slowed and he approached her tentatively, as if he sensed that something was wrong.

"Come here, Merlin," she called, walking toward him. She stretched out her arm, wanting to hold the cat against her chest and listen to him purr, but Merlin turned and ran away. Tears flooded her eyes. She wished she had someone to talk to. She could call Sara, but Sara confided in Marty and Marty was protecting Richard's job. She didn't know what he would do if he learned of Richard's behavior.

Some women would turn to their mothers for comfort, but that wasn't an option. She could imagine what Audrey's reaction would be—a rehash of Clare's father's infidelities. Each time Audrey told the story it was as if Clare had never heard it before, even though she had lived through it—the arguments, the tears, her father's absences, each longer than the last until finally he never returned.

He was a charmer, her father. When he came to pick her up after school, she could hear him wandering the halls, shouting, "Where's the most beautiful girl in the third grade?" She loved him desperately. The last time he returned to their house—did he stay more than a few days?—she would get up early in the morning when she heard his steps in the hall and follow him to the kitchen where she would tell him all about whatever little-girl events in her life she hoped would amuse him. If he wasn't amused, she'd invent more dramatic tales, weaving a skein of stories she hoped would bind him to her so that he wouldn't leave, ever. But he left anyway. Would Richard leave her, too? She had believed he never would; now she wasn't sure. Bile rose in her throat and she swallowed hard, forcing it back down.

One more lap around the garden and then she would try to sit still for a while. The wine didn't seem to be calming her as she had hoped. At the sound of the gate's latch she turned and saw Steve approaching, his crew trailing behind with their tools. Usually, she was glad to see him and the other workers. She enjoyed watching the landscape change day by day. But she didn't want to see Steve today. She didn't want to see anybody at all.

"Hey!"

Clare struggled to appear normal. "Hi."

He came closer. "Is something the matter?" He glanced at her empty wine glass. "You seem … upset."

She shook her head. "I can't talk about it."

Steve hesitated. "Are you sure?"

"I need to be alone right now, Steve." She tried to keep the annoyance out of her voice.

He turned and said something in Spanish to his crew. They began repacking their tools.

"Where are they going?" Clare asked as the workmen filed back towards the gate, a couple of them sneaking sly glances in her direction.

"There's another job they can work on today."

"But they have work to do here," Clare said.

"They can do it tomorrow. You look like you need a break today." He put one arm around her shoulders and turned her toward the house. "Let's go inside."

"I don't want to go inside," Clare said. She knew she sounded like a petulant child but she couldn't help it.

"Listen," Steve whispered into her ear, causing her to shiver, "I'll just refill your wine glass and then I'll leave. Okay?"

Another glass of wine did sound like a good idea; then she could take a nap before the boys got home from school. Naps always restored her; she would often wake up with a fresh perspective. She nodded and let Steve lead her like an invalid into the house, to the kitchen table. He poured her a second full glass of Chardonnay then, as she sipped it, stepped behind her chair and massaged her shoulders.

Clare considered protesting, but his touch felt so good and her shoulders were tense. She closed her eyes and let her mind wander.

"Do you like that?" Steve asked.

"Mmmhmm." She took another sip, then leaned on the table, resting her head on her arms. The wine was finally taking effect and she let herself drift. Steve's hands explored her back, seeking out areas where she held tension, then probing with his strong fingers until the tension melted away and she began to feel warm and relaxed.

"Does that make you feel good ? Do you want more?" Steve whispered. He touched her hair, her cheek, the nape of her neck.

"Yes," she said. She pushed her chair aside and turned, clinging to him. His shirt smelled pure and clean.

"You are so beautiful," Steve said.

She turned her face to his. His lips were full and soft. Her heart began pounding—it had been such a long time since she'd felt that—and the urgency was nearly unbearable.

"Please, please," she heard herself say, and he responded by pressing against her until she felt as if she would faint from pure pleasure. All she could hear was the sound of their breathing.

"Where can we go?" Steve asked, loosening his hold on her. Clare felt suddenly disoriented, dizzy from the wine and the need to make a decision. She groped for his hand and led him out of the kitchen, past the staircase, to the spare room. It was on the north side of the house, and its darkness and chill hit her like a slap. She looked with dismay at the stacks of unpacked boxes lining an entire wall. She had avoided dealing with this room for weeks, unable to unpack one more box.

She felt Steve's warm hands on her shoulders as he steered her towards the unmade bed, the bed she and Richard bought when they moved in to their first apartment sixteen years ago. At the sight of it, she felt a stab of regret: regret for that hopeful young couple who had bought the bed on shaky credit, regret for the damage they had done to their marriage since, regret that it was Steve in this room with her—Steve, not Richard, who was stripping off his jeans, preparing to make love to her.

"I've wanted this ever since I met you," Steve said, pulling her closer. He slid his hands under her shirt. They were roughened from physical labor, his touch very different from Richard's. In the neighbor's yard, a lawn mower started up with a roar, the noise increasing and then drifting away as it passed below and beyond the bedroom window. Steve slipped her off blouse, then her bra, then pulled her close. A car door slammed outside and then the doorbell rang. Jannie? UPS? Clare tensed, but Steve held her and said, "Relax. The door's locked." The bell rang again, then after a moment they heard the sound of a car or truck pulling away.

Clare took a step back and hugged her chest, shivering. The room was quite cold.

"I'm not sure I can do this." She turned and saw that Steve had stepped out of his jockeys. Despite her distress, she was impressed at how completely comfortable—how practiced—he was at stripping off all his clothes in front of a woman.

"Hey. Come on, now."

He sat on the bed and pulled her onto his lap, nuzzling her neck. His breath was a little off. As Steve massaged her shoulders with his strong fingers, he murmured that he didn't mean to rush her. She closed her eyes and let him ease her onto her back, but then their bodies were in an awkward position—half on the bed and half off. She and Richard would have laughed; there would have been no hesitation or strangeness. She wondered if, when he was making love to those other women, Richard ever had these sorts of thoughts, if he ever yearned, as she did, for their comfortable familiarity.

The neighbor's mower was making another deafening pass, drowning out whatever Steve was saying. He took her hand and began to slide it down his torso, from his chest through the brush of hair on his abs to the thicket below. She jerked her hand away.

Steve reached over and stroked her face. "It's all right," he whispered. It was the kind of meaningless assurance you'd give a child. Anger rose in her throat and she sat up.

"No, I don't think it is all right."

"Why not? It's perfectly natural."

"Not natural for me. I can't—I won't—do this. I have a husband and kids."

"A crazy husband," Steve snickered.

Clare pushed him away and began gathering her clothes.

"Maybe. Maybe he is crazy, but I'm not."

CHAPTER EIGHTEEN

THE FOLLOWING MONDAY, CLARE BEGAN PREPARING FOR RICHARD'S RETURN. IT was difficult to know what to do other than stock up on food in case she wasn't able to leave him alone at first. Marty had already arranged for legal work to be dropped off at the house, more as a way to increase Richard's confidence than to reduce the office workload.

She thought all this through while taking a long morning shower, the best time for thinking clearly. When she finished and was toweling herself dry, instead of averting her eyes as she usually did, she leaned close to the bathroom's full-length mirror. Her skin was dry, crosshatched with lines that hadn't been there before. The sun had lightened her hair a little but not enough to camouflage the one-inch underbrush of gray. It might be weeks before she'd have the time to get it colored. She wondered if she could get a last-minute appointment at her mother's salon.

"Oh my God, would you look at that hair!" That had been Audrey's greeting when she showed up unexpectedly at Clare's door the previous Saturday.

"Is that Grandma?" Adam called.

"I came as soon as I heard," Audrey continued, brushing past Clare and into Adam's outstretched arms. "Hello, Sweetie," she said. Audrey never could keep the names of her grandsons straight and so had begun calling them both "Sweetie." Audrey straightened up and shook her head in Clare's direction.

"You know I'll never lie to you, and I must say, you look terrible. You used to keep yourself up—manicures and highlights. What's wrong with you?"

"Now, Audrey," Chuck began.

"Mother!" Two minutes with her mother, and Clare was an angry fifteen-year-old again. She glanced over her shoulder to make sure Adam was out of earshot. "You know I've been a little busy lately, visiting Richard at the Center almost every day, then rushing back to pick up the boys. Richard's very depressed."

"Is it any wonder? It can't do anything for his spirits, with you looking like you do." Audrey enveloped her in a hug and gave her three hundred dollars and the name of a day spa in Beverly Hills that would "fix you right up. Tell them you're my daughter."

~⊙

Two phone calls later—one to Sara asking her to be there when the boys got home from school and then to stay for dinner, the second to the salon—Clare was swathed in a soft robe and led to the spa's manicure salon by Christy, who introduced herself as "the nails lady." As she ran water into the tub for the pedicure, Christy kept up a steady stream of chatter about the O.J. Simpson trial. Since his acquittal, it seemed that the whole city, even the entire country, was reviewing the case's every detail. "Nicole came in here from time to time. The nicest girl you'd ever want to meet. A big tipper, too." She nodded meaningfully at Clare and began to unwrap a sterile pack of pedicure implements. "I just love your mother," Christy said. "She comes all the way up from

San Diego for my pedicures." She eased Clare's feet into the warm water and turned a knob to create a whirlpool effect and vibration of Clare's chair at the same time.

"You have pretty feet," she told Clare, who doubted this was true. Except for babies' feet, which were cute and looked like little bakery buns, feet were really quite improbable looking.

"Why do you say that?"

"Well, you don't have any bunions. Your arches are high. I can tell you buy good shoes." Clare smiled. Shoes were her weakness. She had lost count of how many pairs she owned, and she kept extra shoes in the back of the van, in case she wanted to change. Christy moved to a small footstool opposite and began drying Clare's right foot, holding it in her lap. She nattered on about the details of the trial, Kato somebody, so ceaselessly and boringly that Clare gave up listening and resorted to making sympathetic noises at what she hoped were appropriate moments. After a while, it seemed that the subject had changed. Christy was no longer on O.J. but back to Clare's mother.

"Oh, yes, we get the biggest kick out of her around here."

Clare studied the top of Christy's curly round head. She suddenly had an urge, or maybe it was just a vision, of pushing forward violently with her foot, knocking Christy backwards off the stool onto the floor. She imagined the noise the fall would make, the look of utter shock on Christy's face as she lay on her back, kicking like an oversized beetle. Clare squeezed her eyes shut for a moment, afraid she might give in to the urge. Christy raised her head abruptly, as if she sensed something, but her smile was warm and confiding.

"Doesn't that feel nice?" she asked sweetly. "Now it's time for your cut and color."

⁓◦

"Aunt Sara! Watch this!" Adam cannonballed into the pool, splashing water on two squealing little boys, friends from school, who promptly copied him. Sara wondered if she should move her chair back a little but decided against it, opting to catch the last rays of sunlight. She couldn't remember when Adam started calling her "Aunt Sara," and she wasn't about to ask him why.

All she knew was that it made her happier than she could have imagined.

In the past couple of weeks, she had taken to dropping in on Clare and the boys late in the afternoon. It seemed to comfort all of them. Until she met Clare, Sara hadn't had a close friend with children. Most of her acquaintances who had kids befriended other moms they ran into regularly; they didn't have time to seek out a childless widow who didn't share their carpool and babysitter problems. Clare wasn't like those women. Sure, her boys were older and could be left alone for short periods of time, but it was more than that. Clare knew how to be a friend, even in her present circumstances. She had a gift for friendship and Sara enjoyed being the beneficiary.

When Clare got home, she found Sara making dinner with the boys,.

"Wow! I love your hair!" Sara exclaimed.

"Me too." It was a fabulous haircut, Clare thought, and would require little effort. Her hair ended just below her jawline and could easily be tucked behind her ears, pulled into a short ponytail, or brushed forward to frame her face. The stylist gave her a few wispy bangs "to hide those worry lines," he said, fluffing the fringe with his fingers, reminding Clare how much she loved gay men.

"It's shiny," Adam said. "You look pretty, Mom."

After dinner, when the boys were doing their homework, Clare and Sara dawdled over dessert and coffee.

"Do you feel like you're ready for Richard to come home?" Sara asked.

"I don't know. Sometimes. I worry about all of it—how the boys will do with Richard the way he is. I guess I'll take it day by day. I don't know how else I can cope."

"You'll have to be with him a lot. Is there something you can do for yourself at the same time?"

"I've been thinking about that. I think I know what I'll do."

Clare hummed as she arranged an easel and a table with tubes of paint and pencils on the bedroom balcony. It was a pleasant space overlooking the yard, the house-pocked hillsides of Agave and the smooth, chamois-tinted ridge beyond. On the deck floor beside her was the one box in the garage she cared about. Earlier in the day, she had shifted the containers until she found it: "CK – Personal," its tag read. CK—Clare Kemper, the woman she used to be. The tape on the cardboard lid was stiff and brown, stippled with dust and hair from a dog dead ten years. Inside, a scattering of mouse droppings mingled with boxes of charcoal and sticks of oil pastels. Squinting in the sunlight, she leafed through a thick pad of sketches of Richard and line drawings of her roommates, Martha and Jenny. The likenesses of Richard were particularly good; passion fueled her talent then. And it was talent. The drawings were skillful; in a few brisk strokes she had captured his essence. She remembered how satisfying the act of drawing had been for her all those years ago. She held up another sketch of Richard, angling it to catch the light. It would be a pleasure to paint again. Richard was coming home in two days; trying to recapture her joy in art would help her get through whatever lay ahead.

CHAPTER NINETEEN

CLARE WOKE AT 5:00 A.M. SHE EASED RICHARD'S ARM OFF HER WAIST AND GENTly pushed herself to a sitting position, trying not to disturb him. He would awaken soon enough. She could tell from his breathing, in those few seconds as he struggled to the surface of consciousness, if it was going to be a good day or a bad one. On a good day, he could, with her help, dress himself and go downstairs. On a bad day, he didn't get out of bed.

She kept a record in the same notebook she brought to every meeting with Selva, plotting the course of Richard's depression to help the psychiatrist adjust his medication to achieve some semblance of normality. She didn't know if her notes were useful for the doctor but they mattered to her. She had begun to decorate their margins with vines—passion flower, wisteria and clematis. She liked the way she could curl them through the text. They softened the harshness of the words:

> *October 24, 1995: too tired to get out of bed this morning.*
> *Somewhat better in the p.m. Sat at dinner table with the boys but did not eat.*
> *October 26, 1995: Dressed self and sat outside by the pool for approx. ½ hour. Sat with him.*

She left out the terror. She sat outside with him because she was afraid that if she didn't, he would drown himself. She had become his guardian.

As if he knew, even when he was unconscious, that she was watching over him, willing his recovery, Richard reached out in his sleep, trying to find her. Clare stroked his hair. It was shorter now; they had cut it at the Center right before he left. His natural reddish brown hair was nearly half an inch long, but the rest of his hair was still black from dye. It was an interesting effect— kind of like the woolly bear caterpillars so common in the fall. Clare pulled the blanket up over Richard's bare shoulder. The Titan of Trusts. She had relied on him to be the strong one and now that had all changed. She missed that young law student whose strength and authority had drawn her to him.

It was 1973, the first heavy rain of the year, and she was in the middle of midterm exams at Berkeley. As she hurried across Sproul Plaza towards Sather Gate, winds blowing a four-day storm in over the Pacific whipped her umbrella to shreds, and she was so tired from studying, so discouraged and desolate at the thought of what a new umbrella would cost, that she started to cry. Without warning, the umbrella was stripped from her hand and stuffed into a trash can. She wiped the rain off her face and looked up, astonished.

"I can fix this," the tall young man with reddish brown hair said firmly. "Come with me." When she hesitated, he smiled down at her and asked,

"Are you late for class?"

She shook her head. "I was going to the Library."

"Not without an umbrella," he grinned. "Watch this."

The University police offices were in the basement of Sproul Hall on the Bancroft Avenue side, down a few stone steps from the Plaza. Clare followed the young man and stood silent as he stepped up to the counter.

"My friend here has lost her umbrella," he said, leaning on the counter confidentially, smiling at the police officer. Clare could see piles of lost umbrellas poking from cubby holes along the back wall.

"Yeah?" the cop turned to Clare. "What's it look like?"

She froze. She had never lied or stolen in her life.

"It's black with a wooden handle," the boy beside her said.

The cop smiled at Clare.

"You're sure? Black with a wooden handle?"

She nodded. The policeman ambled across the small office, pulling various black umbrellas out of cubbies.

"This one?" he asked.

"No," the boy said, and when the cop turned his back, he whispered to Clare, "Reject a few."

"No," she said to the next one. The third. She would go for the third choice. That would be convincing.

"That's it!" she said, and her new-found friend nodded in approval at the third black umbrella with the wooden handle. She could feel his raincoat brush against hers.

The police officer winked at her as he handed the umbrella across the counter. "Stay dry, kids," he said.

Outside, the young man laughed, delighted.

"Wasn't that easy?" he asked.

"Honestly," she said, exasperated.

"Oh, I'm not sure that's the word I'd use," the boy replied, and he laughed again. He had a wonderful laugh—loud, hearty. It made her laugh, too. "This calls for a celebration. Your first successful heist." He looked at his watch. "I know a great place. Want a cup of coffee?"

She hesitated. She had already missed fifteen minutes of study time. But maybe it wouldn't hurt, just this once, to take an hour off and find out what this boy was like. He was cute, she decided, in a large-scale, brash way. She had, up until this moment, preferred smaller men; they seemed more sensitive.

They ran through the rain to the intersection of Bancroft and Telegraph, and crossed the street. She assumed they were heading towards The Med or one of the other coffee shops that lined Telegraph Avenue. Instead, he turned up the hill and she followed him a few steps up Bancroft, past the smoke shop, then stopped as he took out his keys and unlocked double glass doors to an apartment building.

She backed away. "I can't," she said. He turned, looking at her intently. After a moment, he held out his hand for her to shake. "I'm Richard Stone." He pointed to the name on the strip by the apartment numbers next to the door buzzer.

"See?" This is the closest place, without getting soaked," he said. "And I make really, really good coffee." He grinned and she began to waver. "Look, I'm as respectable as they come, I swear." He held up his right hand, as if he were taking an oath. "I'm at Boalt Law School—third year, almost done. Connecticut Yankee, Yale undergrad. I have very good manners. I promise I'll make you the best cup of coffee you've ever had—that's all—and escort you right back out this door."

She loved coffee. But what would her mother say? What if this handsome guy were a psychopath? An axe murderer? But he was a law student.

"You can trust me," he said, pushing the door open. "Come on."

She followed him through the double glass doors, feeling, as she often did in those days, that something important was about to happen.

~○

And something had happened. An attachment for the flimsiest of reasons: neither was involved with anyone at the time; they both liked strong coffee; she admired his self-assurance, he was drawn to her timidity; she relied on his strength, he cherished her need for protection. They were little more than children then, but they clung to each other, made a life and a family, and arrived at this place and this predicament: a man in a bed, clutching his wife as he slept.

She absently stroked his head, thinking how easy it was to be patient with him at times when he looked so vulnerable, and how hard it was to deal with him when he was awake. Living with a clinically depressed person takes a heavy toll, Selva had warned her. She had no idea what he meant then, but now she did. No matter how many times she told herself that this was an illness, as real as any other serious disease, it was hard to sympathize with depression, which made Richard particularly unreasonable and self-centered. If he had cancer, she thought she could understand his pain. But to watch him—intelligent, prosperous, well-loved, with an enviable life—drag around as if there were something special about his suffering was infuriating. Ten or twelve times a day, just the sight of him with his head drooping, his face contorted by his "poor me" expression, caused such an eruption of rage within her that she wanted to kick him, punch him, scream at him to get on with his life, to stop being so self-involved.

Richard stirred and turned his head.

"Hey," he said softly.

"Hey."

Richard reached up and touched Clare's head. "I miss your hair," he complained. And I miss you, she thought but did not say.

He put his head in her lap and curled into a fetal position, one arm wrapped around her hip. As she rubbed his back, she thought of that brash and charming boy walking beside her across Sproul Plaza in Berkeley. Was he manic then? Were all those occasions when he was particularly joyful, when it seemed that everyone he met was drawn to him—was that really Richard or was that his mania? And who was he now—this dried-out husk? She wondered how much of what she loved in him was real and if that part would return.

CHAPTER TWENTY

It was strange to be back home. Richard felt unsure of himself, even unsteady on his feet. The staircase was twice as tall as he remembered and the act of climbing it was difficult to manage. The boys treated him like a distant relative. Matt turned his face away when he caught Richard looking at him; Adam slowly came around, like a cat checking out a houseguest. That's what it was. He felt like a guest in his own house; neither home nor mind nor body fully belonged to him anymore.

The heaviness in his chest on awakening increased with every hour to the point that he could hardly breathe. It took an act of will to get out of bed and often he couldn't manage it. Marty sent Diana over once or twice a week with papers for him to review, but he was incapable of concentrating until the sun had passed overhead. At some point in late afternoon, the fog that enveloped him all morning would dissipate—not entirely, but enough for him to move downstairs—and he would spend part of an hour staring at legal documents, the rest of the afternoon in front of the television with the boys. It wasn't much, but it was the best he could do. While the screen flickered in front of them and Matt made cynical remarks that Adam found hilarious, Richard would think back to his life before September, to all the things he had been and could do, now lost, perhaps permanently. He wasn't sure he would be able to go back to work for Phil and Marty; he didn't have the mental acuity or the energy. He had lost his edge. He couldn't even drive. Who can live in Los Angeles without driving? Grief would engulf him then, and he would begin the slow climb up the stairs to the bedroom.

Too often, though he was exhausted, sleep did not come at night. He lay in bed listening to the counterpoint of Clare's breathing and the moan of the wind against the windows, forcing itself through cracks in the caulk. He imagined himself bending against its force, struggling across the bleakness, towards the sanity that he was told lay on the other side of depression.

Richard blinked as he entered the kitchen from the patio. The house seemed dark and murky after the flat November sun of the yard. He called for Clare, but there was no answer. The clock said 1:00 p.m. He couldn't remember how long he had been outside. Another stack of papers was piled neatly on the table and he ran his thumb along its edge. Diana must have come by. He slumped into a kitchen chair, exhausted. He would need to lie down for a while so he could stay awake after the boys got home. Tucking the papers under his arm, he scuffed slowly through the house to the stairs, then realized he was too tired to make it all the way up. He sat down heavily on the bottom step, trying to puzzle out a solution. He placed the documents three steps up, then pulled himself along on hands and knees, using the railing for support, until he reached the stack of files. He placed the pile another few stairs away, then repeated the process. Ten minutes later, he had made it to the top, where he thought he would rest a little before crawling into the bedroom.

When Clare came home, she saw that Richard was no longer on the patio, where she had left him only half an hour ago. She quickly checked the pool: no body floating in the cool, turquoise water. Rushing to the foyer, she looked up and was startled to see Richard, on his side, on the landing outside their bedroom. She hurried up the staircase, calling his name, and dropped to her knees beside him. When he stirred and opened his eyes, she fought the impulse to slap him.

"What are you doing? You scared me!"

"Sorry," Richard answered. He didn't look sorry. "I was just taking a little rest before I went back to bed."

"Oh, for God's sake!" Clare snapped, yanking at his arm. "Get up."

Richard slowly pushed himself onto all fours, then held onto her for support as he pulled himself to his knees. Clare stumbled, then regained her balance. At the sound of the front door slamming, she looked down into the foyer at Matt. His head was shaved bald. Matt stalked up the stairs, and stood for a moment, glaring at his parents.

"What happened?" Richard asked, lifting his head.

"What do you care?" Matt muttered, trying to edge past his father's kneeling form. Richard lunged, exhibiting more energy than he had in weeks, and tackled Matt, bringing him down to the floor beside him.

"Don't you dare talk to me like that," Richard said between gritted teeth. Clare could see the muscles of his jaw working and wondered if he was going to hit the boy. She reached down and put a restraining hand on his shoulder.

"Of course we care," Richard said. "What are you—crazy?"

At that, Matt rose and Clare could see that his face was red with fury. "No, you're the one who's crazy," he spat out.

"I am NOT crazy!" Richard yelled after him. "I'm not!"

~⊂⊃

"Matt's having a hard time," Clare told Marty when he stopped by that night to visit Richard. "He's shaved his head and he's hanging out with some bad kids."

Marty nodded. "Does he know anything about carpentry?"

"Do you?"

"Hey, I'm learning! I'm working on a little project at my place—just fooling around, trying to build a deck off the bedroom. Maybe the kid could help me."

It was hard for Clare to imagine Matt doing any physical labor. Just to get him to mow the lawn—with a power mower, for heaven's sake—was an ordeal. He would come inside for water and a rest every ten minutes, stretching a one-hour job into three. But working at Marty's would give Matt some measure of independence in a safe place with an adult who wasn't his parent. It might work.

~⌒

Matt scuffed along the top of the wall, poking at the chaparral with a dried branch. He might have heard a hiss in response to his prodding, but he wasn't sure. Rattlesnakes were cagey; they could spring out of nowhere and surprise you. Up the hill, something brown burst into the open and Matt could see a roadrunner standing alert and alarmed, fixing him with a single beady eye before it ran, clicking noisily, into the scrub. After all those years of watching them in cartoons, he had expected roadrunners would really go "beep beep" instead of "click click." He wondered what else he had always believed that wasn't true.

He picked his way up the steep slope, stepping only in clear places far from rocks and underbrush where the snakes might lie, waiting to strike at him. At the sound of an engine, he turned and saw his parents' car on Grey Rock Road, far below, approaching their garage. They would be wondering where he was and why he hadn't come home from school yet. They would never dream he was way up here, on the forbidden side of the wall, looking down on them.

Matt hunched in the dry weeds and waited for Jonah, who was already fifteen minutes late. That was the trouble with Jonah; he was a flake. But Jonah was so mysterious; something about the way he put things kept Matt interested. Today Jonah passed him a note in Algebra suggesting they meet here, that he'd bring something that Matt would really like, something that "would be worth the wait." Matt wondered if it was marijuana. He liked it the times he'd tried it. Or maybe pills of some kind? Pills might be a problem, might make him sleepy or so high that he couldn't control his actions, and then his parents would notice something was wrong. But it would take a lot to get them to notice, they were so focused on Dad these days. Not that he didn't need the attention. His father seemed to have shrunk over the past month. Matt knew he was getting taller—nearly five foot nine last time he measured himself against the closet door—but his father seemed to have become smaller, bent-over and droopy. He heard his mother telling Sara that whatever was wrong with his father can be hereditary. So would he turn into his father someday—a man who ran away from his family, then came back smaller and so changed that he didn't want to be with his own kids anymore?

Matt waited for Jonah another half hour and then gave up. He could see the landscaping crew piling into their trucks far below him. That meant it was almost dinnertime, and his parents would wonder where he was. If he went home now, there wouldn't be so many questions. A rush of air to his right, then a shadow, as a red-tailed hawk swooped low into the grass, grabbing a field mouse and ascending again, its broad wings flapping. Matt's heart raced. He could swear the hawk had glared at him. "Fuck you!" he yelled, and whacked his branch on the ground until it snapped.

~○

Bob returned from his month in Cabo San Lucas and phoned Richard, as he had promised. Richard was grateful for his calls, which came regularly— once a week on Wednesdays—though he knew he didn't sound grateful. Bob seemed to ignore that, to look past the grunted responses and the flat tone of voice.

"I'm going to take you out for coffee," Bob announced one day, ignoring Richard's protest that he didn't feel like leaving the house. "Won't know till you try it," Bob said. An hour later, he was at their doorstep and ten minutes after that they were at Java City in Westlake Village, sitting at a corner table.

"How long does it take to feel better?" Richard asked, staring into his coffee. "I keep waiting for signs of improvement."

"Maybe you're waiting for the wrong signs," Bob answered, swizzling fake sugar through the foam of his double cappuccino. He was tanned and fit from his sojourn at Cabo San Lucas. "You're not going to feel like you do now on one day and then get up and play tennis the next. It's gradual. Slow. Two steps forward, one step back."

Richard raised his head.

"You grew up in New England? Right?" Bob asked. When Richard nodded, he continued. "Remember how it was when spring was coming? You'd have a good day, or a run of good days, when it got warmer and you could smell the soil—that great smell that comes with the spring thaw? And then one morning you'd wake up and there'd be snow again, and you'd feel like you'd lost ground: spring would never come. But it always did. It just came slowly. Warm days, cold days: good days, bad days. Increments."

Richard rubbed his face hard with his palms; he did this often now, making sure he was still there. "I don't know if there are any good days," he said.

"Okay. Let me show you something that works for me," Bob said, flattening his napkin on the tabletop and pulling out a pen. He drew a grid with three headings across the top: Then/Now/What Helps. Along the left-hand side of the grid, he listed categories: Sleep, Conversation, Reading.

"Now. Let's talk about sleep. What was it like before?"

"I couldn't sleep. You know that," Richard answered, irritated.

"And now?"

"I still can't sleep on my own."

"But you do get some sleep?"

"Yeah, but with sleeping pills," Richard answered warily. "And sometimes with other stuff."

"Like?"

"Like I don't take a nap during the day, and I stay up till about midnight."

"And then you can get to sleep?"

"Yeah. For only a few hours."

"But you sleep."

"Yeah." Richard wondered why he felt so grudging; there was improvement, he could see that.

"Okay." Bob filled in the grid under the "Then/Now/What Helps" headings. "It's the same with the other categories. Can you get through a conversation now? Obviously, because you're talking to me. You told me before you couldn't talk to Marty when he came over." He nodded and took up his pen again, filling in the squares.

"So you get the point? You aren't where you want to be, you're not where you're going to be, but you're getting there."

"Try leaning into it," Marty suggested, and Matt pressed his weight against the power drill, pushing as hard as he could to drive the drill bit into the deck support.

"You got it." Marty patted his shoulder. "Now let's eat. You can finish that after lunch."

Matt liked these Saturday projects, and he liked the way his muscles were sore at the end of the day; he could actually watch them grow from week to week. It was awesome, how different Marty was from his dad. Marty didn't boss you around, didn't act like a know-it-all, and besides that, he was nice. Marty was always glad to see you and didn't ask prying questions. He treated you like an adult. Marty's refrigerator was always full of cool stuff—sodas and Chinese food. He didn't care about how many cokes Matt drank in a day or any of the other things his parents got on him about.

"Whatcha been up to?" Marty asked. Even though his father might ask the same thing, it didn't bother Matt when Marty questioned him.

He shrugged. "The usual. School, homework, soccer. You know."

"You like it here?"

"You mean your house?"

Marty laughed. "No, I mean Los Angeles."

Matt made a face and shrugged again. "I guess it's okay." He thought about it for a while and added, "The music's good. You get to hear the new stuff earlier than in Alameda."

Marty nodded. "Yeah. The music scene's big in LA." They picked through the cartons of cold Chinese leftovers.

"I've got this friend," Matt said. "Jonah." He waited for Marty to say something. Surely his parents had told him. They made no secret of their dislike for Jonah, with his shaved head and eyebrow rings. When Marty didn't respond, Matt continued, "My Dad doesn't like him. Neither does my Mom. But he's not so bad, really, and he's an awesome guitar player. He could be professional, he's so good."

"What kind of guitar?"

"He plays bass. He's better than Chris Novoselic."

"Why don't your folks like him?"

Matt set his moo shu pork down and took a gulp of soda before he answered. "They think he's a bad influence on me because his parents sort of let him do whatever he wants."

"Is he? A bad influence?"

"Naw." It was so easy to be patient with Marty and so hard with his parents. "He's just a little flaky, that's all."

"Flaky how?"

"You know. A bullshitter." Now that was something else he'd never get by with at home—using words like "bullshit."

"Like once, he told me he'd meet me at the top of the hill across from our house? And I waited for an hour? He never came. He kind of led me on with the story about how the wait would be worth it, you know. But the next day he just blew me off. He said he thought I knew he was joking. I was really pissed."

"But you can count on him for the important stuff," Marty remarked.

"I don't know." Matt thought about the times Jonah had let him down, then made it up by loaning him his guitar. You couldn't count on him, really. That was what he didn't like about Jonah. He'd never thought of that before.

"It's important to be able to count on your friends," Marty said as he rose to clear his plate.

"What about you?" Matt asked, trying not to sound angry.

Marty turned, a puzzled half smile on his face. "You think you can't count on me?"

Matt's anger was quickly displaced by dismay. Marty was one of the few people in the world he could count on. "I meant my dad," he said. "He's your friend and you can't count on him."

Marty placed his thick, stubby hands flat on the granite countertop and stared at them as if their pattern of freckles and black hair contained the response he was seeking. "That's a tough one, isn't it? I've thought about it a lot because it is hard; it's hard for you and your mother and Adam, it's hard for your dad's friends. Because of his illness, your father is unpredictable." He smiled suddenly. "He was always unpredictable—it's one of the things I love about him—but before September he stayed within the boundaries. Whatever 'boundaries' are." Marty raised both hands and made little quotation marks with his index fingers. "Now all that's changed. The medication dampens him down but if he lets up on it, he could go over the edge again. All kinds of stuff can throw him off. If he doesn't sleep he's in danger. It's a bitch."

Marty faced Matt. "Here's the way I look at it. Manic depression is an illness—not like the illnesses we're used to thinking about, but still an illness. Now if your dad had asthma, I wouldn't expect him to be running marathons. Most days we could probably hike up a mountain, but some days his asthma would be in control of him, and he couldn't even take a walk, forget running a marathon with me."

Matt unsuccessfully tried to suppress a smile at the thought of Marty's running a marathon.

"Yeah, yeah, I know," Marty laughed. "Bad example. But follow along with me here. If your dad had asthma, I couldn't count on him to be able to exert himself at the same level every day. Some days asthma would affect how he functioned. Your dad has a mood disorder and it affects how he functions and sometimes I can't count on him. But we don't give up on our friends just because they're sick now and then, do we?" He answered his own question, shaking his head. "I can tell from day to day when I can count on your dad and when I can't. On the days when I can't count on him, I kind of put him in a little park in my imagination. I just settle him on a bench there and let him rest the way I would a friend with asthma. I let him catch his breath."

Richard woke and lay still, waiting for the heaviness to descend onto his chest, signaling that another interminable day had begun. This morning, though, the sensation of being knocked flat, the feeling of utter emptiness was missing. Instead, Richard noticed the chatter of Clare and the boys downstairs and the smell of coffee. He sighed and pulled the sheet tight under his chin. This was such a waste: the long, boring, somnolent days, the restless nights, the uncertainty about the future. He yearned for his old life, for Clare to be happy and his sons glad to see him. He thought of what he missed most: Matt's soccer games on autumn Saturdays; watching Sunday Morning in bed with Clare; the smell of Adam's hair; a fresh yellow legal pad. Instead of the familiar feeling of hopelessness that usually engulfed him, he felt a faint stirring. When Clare checked on him half an hour later, he surprised her by being showered and dressed.

CHAPTER TWENTY-ONE

Richard had the feeling that the ground was moving beneath him as he strode across the familiar carpet on his first day back in the office. He had arrived early. Why not? He couldn't sleep. And this would be an opportunity to impress Phil with his commitment to the firm. The shaking continued and he glanced at the hanging light fixtures, as most Californians did, to see if they were swaying from an earthquake. They weren't. The quake was in his head. He thought that on the whole he was doing a good job of fooling the staff. He had psyched himself up in the parking lot so that he could walk into the office armed with an imitation of his former self-confidence. A few of the young attorneys—real go-getters, already at their desks at 7:00 a.m.—had come out to greet him, applauding. Wait until he told Clare that one! He had carried it off, acting as if he was, indeed, the Richard Stone they all knew.

He arranged his face in a broad smile and strode into Phil's office. His partner rose and took Richard's hand.

"Welcome back," Phil said. "We've missed you."

Liar. You think I'm crazy, don't you? Richard thought, smiling and nodding. "It's great to be back," he said. "I'm ready to get down to business."

"Well, I'm glad to hear that."

Richard sat in one of the chairs on the other side of Phil's desk and waited, but Phil was busy moving his pens around and straightening stacks of papers.

"How's Maria?"

"Great, great." Phil clasped his hands together and placed them on top of one of the stacks, then looked up at Richard.

"And Clare? How's Clare doing?"

"She's fine, Phil."

"And the boys?"

"Never better." Richard was determined to wait Phil out, matching him nicety for nicety, cliché for cliché

"So," Phil said. He rubbed his hands together, then rose. Apparently he had exhausted his limited supply of bonhomie and wanted Richard out of there.

"I won't keep you," Phil added. "I know you have a lot of work to do."

⌒◯

At his desk for the first time since September, Richard felt another surge of uncertainty. He doubted he could resurrect his old life and former talents. He turned his nameplate around so he could look at it, to remind himself of who he had been: Richard Stone, the Titan of Trusts. He quailed at the thought that he would be discovered for the pretender he had become.

Diana had obviously prepared for his return. A bud vase holding a silk rose sat squarely in the middle of his desk pad with a "Welcome back!" sign in her childish, rounded hand beneath it. "Inter-Office Memos, Sept. 25–Dec 4," were clipped together to his right; apparently she thought bureaucratic matters should be his first concern. He spun his chair around to view the tall stacks of papers Diana had arranged neatly on the credenza behind him. The towers of documents swam before his eyes and, again, it seemed as if the ground was moving. The stacks were too tall. Too much. He swiveled away from the credenza and waited for the vertigo to subside. One thing at a time, he told himself, wiping perspiration from his forehead with his handkerchief.

He glanced through the office memos to see if they contained anything of note. He realized that the text was barely registering and forced himself to slow down. An hour passed without his noticing; he was relieved to find nothing of importance in the documents.

Soon he would have to deal with the towers behind him, but just thinking about them made his pulse race and he began to hyperventilate. In the old days, when he could work twelve hours straight, as full of energy at 10:00 p.m. as he was when he woke, he could have handled those staggering piles, but no longer. Richard covered his face with both hands and breathed into the dark private space he had created.

He didn't hear the door open and was startled to hear Diana ask,

"Are you all right?"

"Of course!" He dropped his hands and forced a smile. "Just thinking."

"You want some coffee?"

"No, no," Richard said. "Thanks anyway."

"There's someone on the phone for you? Says his name is Bob? Do you want to call him back?"

"No, I'll take it."

Diana nodded and backed out of the office. He wondered what she would tell the others.

Richard grabbed for his phone, grateful that just when he needed him, Bob was there. Like a guardian angel. It was the year of guardian angels. Nicole Brown Simpson's sister had worn a small golden angel pin on her lapel during the murder trial. A lot of good that had done. But since then, hundreds, thousands, of cherubs in every imaginable form had sprouted up in the stores and mail order catalogs. Christmas ornaments of flaxen-haired babies with wings lined the SavOn Drug Store aisles. Plaster *putti* dangled from the ceilings of gift shops, smiling serenely down on customers.

"Bob?" Richard whispered.

"Yeah. Why are you whispering?"

It poured out of him: the fear, the false bravado, the impossible stacks of work. Bob listened, not interrupting until Richard began to repeat himself, his anxiety propelling him into a spin.

"Okay," Bob said. "Slow down. Here's what I do. It helps. Divide the big stacks into small ones that seem reasonable. Maybe two inches high, maybe four. Pay attention to how you feel when you look at them. You'll know if they need to be made smaller."

It seemed so stupid, Richard thought, making baby bits out of work he could have gotten through with ease only months ago. Still, he was desperate. Even looking at the stacks of paper made him crazy.

"It's a way of getting through it," Bob said. "Pretty soon you won't need to do that."

Take it one task at a time, Richard counseled himself. Stay calm. He split the tallest stack into four smaller ones, swiveled his chair around so he didn't have to look at the rest of them, and began to read Small Stack One. From time to time, he looked up from the documents and read his nameplate: Richard Stone. Still here.

"You're sure of this," the doctor said—a statement rather than a question.

"Yes. Of course."

Richard sat in the chair opposite Dr. Selva.

"And she was how old, did you say?"

"Thirty-seven." Richard closed his eyes and rubbed his forehead with his fingertips.

"And there was heart disease in her family?"

"I don't know. I never knew my grandparents. She was German and an orphan. She didn't talk about them. I think it must have been painful for her to talk about losing her parents."

"Yes. Losing a parent is painful."

Richard looked past Selva's shoulder, out the window, to the dripping foliage beyond. He remembered walking with his mother in her garden. He was very young, perhaps three years old, or four. She pointed at different flowers and he called out the names she had taught him.

"Jacob's Ladder! Angel's Trumpet! Love Lies Bleeding!"

His mother laughed and clapped her hands, delighted.

"And what's your favorite?"

"Kiss Me Over the Garden Gate!" he crowed.

She lifted his small body and swung him in a wide arc, then put him down and kissed him. It was sunny that day.

Another day, many other days in the years that followed, he came home from school to a darkened house. In the deep of Connecticut winter, darkness fell at 4:00 p.m. She would be in her room, the draperies drawn, one arm flung across her eyes. She lifted her head at the sound of his voice, then sank back onto the pillow. She was very, very tired, she said. "Please close the door. That's a good boy."

Sometimes he would hear her whispering to herself, forgetting he was there. "What's the use?" she would croak in a small, dry voice. "What's the use?" He remembered how frightened he had been then, with his father away at work most of the time and his mother lost in her own world, heedless of his existence. "I'm the use," he wanted to tell her.

There was no question of bringing friends home, of course. He didn't want anyone to see how he lived. Not even in the good times. Not even on the days when she was awake when he got home, all the lights in the house blazing, three pies baking in the oven and soup on the stove. Because on those days, in those times of bright lights and bustle, she would talk too loudly, tell off-color jokes to his friends and then ridicule him for his embarrassment. In some ways, he preferred the periods when she took to her darkened bedroom.

"That doesn't make sense, does it?" Richard asked the doctor. "That she would die in her sleep of a heart attack? When she was so young?"

~⌒◦

Richard's mother was beside him; it was late at night and she had wakened him with her touch, the slight brushing of her hand against his hair. His forehead was damp and her hand was cool. That night long ago, he had drifted off to sleep. Later, there was a muffled sound in the hallway outside his door. Voices. Footsteps. He sat up in bed, calling for her, but it was another woman who came to him, Mrs. Tulland, the neighbor across the road. She scooped him up in her arms as if he were a baby instead of a seven-year-old boy and he felt her soft, pillowy bosom, so different from his mother's sharp, bony body, as she carried him downstairs. He remembered that she had paused to grab a knitted blanket from the sofa, then carried him into the dark, cold night to the Tullands' farmhouse across the road. And then came the sound of sirens, setting the dog to howling.

A heart attack. In her sleep, his father told him. She felt no pain.

~◯

"Does that make sense to you?" Richard asked again. "I just ... I never thought of questioning it."

"Of course you didn't. You were a little boy."

"But now I wonder. Do you think? Do you think she could have killed herself?"

Dr. Selva shifted, putting fingertips together to make a tent of his hands. Richard felt a surge of annoyance.

"Have you ever asked your father?"

~◯

Clare decided she would attend the firm's holiday party even though Richard was in Connecticut. She would have at least one person to talk to—Sara, who was coming as Marty's guest. And it would be a good opportunity to check in with Phil Wentworth, just to make sure he wasn't displeased with Richard's unexpected trip.

She put on her best black cocktail dress, highest heels and, as a special treat for herself, paid to have her hair washed and blown dry. She felt great— even beautiful. In confirmation that she might look as good as she felt, Matt had turned his head away and blushed when she twirled in front of the boys and asked, "Well, what do you think?"

Phil's alcohol intake was being closely monitored by his wife, Maria, and while it made him less susceptible to Clare's charms, he would be more likely to remember the encounter, and that was a good thing. Phil held her close just a few seconds too long when she greeted him; Maria, only two feet away, blew her a kiss.

"Richard is so sorry he couldn't be here, Phil."

Wentworth's eyes had wandered to her cleavage. "Yes. He said his father is ill."

Said his father is ill? Did he doubt that Richard was telling him the truth? "That's right," Clare nodded. "His father's health has declined rather quickly this past month, and Richard thought it would be better to go now, when work is slowing because of the holidays, rather than wait until after the first of the year."

Phil narrowed his eyes. "Of course."

This wasn't going as Clare had hoped. She fought back anxiety, wondering how she could steer the conversation to safer ground. She was relieved when Maria rejoined them, a fresh glass of sparkling water in hand.

"I hear you have a beautiful new garden," Maria said.

"Yes, and I'd love for you to see it," Clare gushed. "As a matter of fact"—she was improvising now—"you'll be getting an invitation to a party Richard and I are having in January—a garden party. An afternoon affair, something casual, so you can see the new landscape."

They hadn't seen the old one, but did it matter? Phil brightened a little and even promised they'd come.

"Kind of a 'Welcome to Spring,'" Clare continued.

"But Spring doesn't come until late March," Maria pointed out.

Did she have to be so literal? Clare laughed and waved a hand in the air, one of Richard's gestures. "We're planning an early welcome."

CHAPTER TWENTY-TWO

THE HOUSES IN CONNECTICUT WERE DECORATED FOR CHRISTMAS—A LIGHTED candle in every window. Richard had forgotten that lovely custom. There was a single candle in only one window of his father's house in Sainsbury: the window of what his family used to call the library, now Nathaniel's first-floor bedroom. The girl from the Visiting Nurses put it there, his father said. A hospital bed had been positioned in the bay where his desk once stood. The view was bleakly beautiful.

"I was adamant about the bed's placement," his father said, and Richard smiled. Nathaniel Stone had lost mobility but not acuity, not his vocabulary. When night fell, they watched the evening news together, as they always had. Last year, his father finally bought a new television with a remote control, a concession to his physical limitations, and now he marveled at the device.

"So handy," he said, sounding like a television pitchman. "I can't imagine why I waited so long."

Richard got up at dawn on the first morning of his visit—he had had a difficult night, trying to sleep in an unfamiliar bed. He hoped that the disruption of the time zone change and sleeplessness wouldn't throw his mood off.

He was easily thrown out of kilter, and he needed to be as steady as possible for the task ahead.

Richard's winter boots were still in the mudroom closet; nothing changed in his father's house. He pulled them on, bundled himself up and set out to explore the property and surrounding fields. The plaque by the front door read "Old Stone Tavern," with the inscription below "Nathaniel Stone, 1763." The red clapboard colonial stood a few feet from Route 309, a local road dating back to pre-revolutionary days. "A stop on the road to nowhere," Richard's father liked to say, though it had probably been a farm road to somewhere, connecting small settlements of colonists. It was there, on the edge of a cart track, that the first of the Stones to arrive in New England built his tavern and inn for weary travelers. As a child, Richard had been forbidden to play in front of the house because it was so close to the road, but he had the run of the back fields and the woods beyond. He circled around to the bluestone terrace and watched the sky lighten. The outline of Hedgehog Mountain to the northwest gradually became more distinct.

Between the house and the pond, down a broad slope, his mother's vegetable garden had once stood. His father had continued to plant the plot each spring, though with fewer varieties, until his health worsened. All that was visible of the garden now was a sagging fence. Richard tramped across the frozen lawn and gazed into the winter-blackened rectangle, trying to reconstruct in his mind the neat rows of lettuce, beans, peas and rhubarb that his mother grew. As a child, he had liked to help her in the garden; he enjoyed the days when she was focused enough to spend time there.

"It cures my heebie jeebies," she had told him once, hoeing a row of tomatoes. He smiled at the memory of his first encounter with a seed—it couldn't have been, of course, but that was how he remembered it. It was early summer, and his mother had the idea that a row of sunflowers along the fence would "make a pretty show." She held the seeds out to him casually, not sensing his excitement at the prospect of planting. He remembered what he had expected: round and shiny beads, like cat's eye marbles, with a swirl of orange, yellow and black: something spectacular to match the beauty of the mature plant. Instead, he looked into his palm with disappointment, for all that was there, all she had given him, was a little pile of drab black and white striped seeds. Sunflower seeds.

Before Richard settled into the easy chair beside his father's bed he poured his dad a Scotch, himself a club soda. They were continuing the nightly ritual of a drink with the six o'clock news. His father reached out with one blotched, papery hand and grasped Richard's.

"I'm glad you're here, son."

Once, this would have made Richard uneasy; now it was a comfort.

For the duration of the visit, Richard's father had arranged for Meals on Wheels to leave two dinners each day. They reminded Richard of his elementary school cafeteria food—nutritious, filling and bland. Night was a depressing time for him, standing alone in the familiar kitchen, fiddling with the controls of the temperamental oven his mother had been thrilled to own so many years ago. The damn thing was downright dangerous, he thought, probably leaking gas. He wished he knew more about mechanical devices, wished he had listened to his father's endless explanations of how things worked. But he hadn't, and the closest he came to fixing anything was calling a repairman himself, rather than relying on Clare to do it. He wished he had not agreed to eat these wretched meals, but his father's pride had stopped him from objecting. The old man wanted to demonstrate that he was still the master of his house. Every night of the visit, Richard forked vent holes in the foil of the two dinners, holding his breath so he wouldn't have to smell the stink of the whitefish or soft brown broccoli, and vowed that tomorrow he would have a pizza delivered.

"Dad, I need to ask you something," Richard said. It was the third night of his visit and it was snowing hard. It had been a good day. His father was excited at the prospect of the predicted Nor'easter, and Richard got caught up in his enthusiasm. He had forgotten that feeling of anticipation and the ritual preparations an impending storm involved. The candles, matches and flashlights were ready; wood had been stockpiled next to the three downstairs fireplaces; the bathtub was filled with water. Right on schedule ("For once," Richard's father said, scornful of the new TV weatherman) the storm hit. They watched the harsh landscape soften under a blanket of white and the edges of the rectangular windowpanes melt into ovals

"What is it?" his father asked, his voice querulous. He looked startled, even frightened, not the reaction Richard expected. His father had been a legendary prosecutor in his day, so calm, deliberate and fearless that he had been appointed to a judgeship in the Hartford Superior Court while he was still in his thirties. Now he was a frail and frightened old man.

"It's about Mother. Some things I remembered about her that I want to check with you."

His father shut his eyes and nodded slowly. Was he remembering her this night, savoring their brief time together? Or had he shut his eyes against his son's question, dreading what Richard would ask? Richard could not be certain. This had been true all his life—the ambiguity of emotion in this house, the sense that to be watchful was the only way to figure out what was going on. Richard thought his childhood vigilance was what made him such a perceptive litigator.

"What I remember is that Mother would be in her room when I got home from school. It would be dark in there, and she'd say she was 'resting.' I had to leave her alone and be quiet."

His father nodded.

"Did you know she did that?"

"Yes."

"That wasn't normal, Dad."

"She did the best she could. Your mother struggled much of her adult life with—I don't know how to describe it—some deep sadness. She was a lively, wonderful woman when we met."

With his old man's hands, he folded and refolded a napkin left over from dinner, smoothing it carefully each time, then rolling it into a tight cylinder, unrolling it and beginning the process again. The repetition of the gesture, its obsessive quality, made Richard look away.

"Not that she wasn't always a wonderful woman," his father amended after a long silence, picking up the thread of the conversation where he had misplaced it. "She tried very hard, your mother. She was a considerate person by nature. But sometimes," he shook his head, "she just couldn't cope. And then she'd take to bed, as you remember. It was an illness, a nervous illness."

He undid all the folds of the napkin, smoothed it flat, and rested his hands. They sat in silence, watching the snow fall on the three sides of the bay window, enfolding them in its arms.

"Why are you asking me this now?" his father said. Again, that disconcerting resumption of the conversation as if no time had passed.

Richard cleared his throat. "I had an 'incident,' a few months ago, a sort of 'breakdown,' you could call it."

A range of expression passed over his father's face: confusion, disbelief, sorrow. "You didn't tell me. Clare said you needed some rest."

"You were in the hospital. So was I. It seemed better to wait until I could be here with you." When he had finished telling his father the story of his illness as it had been reconstructed for him, Richard said, "It can run in families. They call it bipolar disorder, or manic depression. I think Mother must have been bipolar, too."

His father covered his eyes with one trembling hand.

"I'll be okay, Dad," Richard continued. "They have medicine for it now. Several medicines. I take a couple. I'm okay, as long as I take the pills." There was no point in telling him about the difficulties with medication, the daily struggle for balance.

"They didn't have anything like that to help her back then," his father said.

"But about Mother—I need to know this—did she—you know—how did she—did she kill herself?" His father winced as if he had been struck.

"Dad? Did she commit suicide?"

His father began smoothing the napkin again, pressing out each wrinkle until he got to the edges of the cloth, then starting again in the middle. The silence indoors was as deep as the silence of the snow outside, and Richard wondered if his father had drifted away, lost in his memories.

"Dad?"

"Yes," his father said softly.

Richard felt himself flush and his heart began to race. He hadn't known and yet he did know after all, it seemed. After a moment he asked, "Did she leave a note?"

His father passed a spotted hand across his eyes and murmured,

"It said something like 'I'm sorry. I can't go on.' I don't remember exactly. Nothing more illuminating than that. When she got into those dark phases, she was nearly incapable of expressing herself."

"Did you keep it?"

His father shook his head. "I couldn't bear to."

"How did she do it?"

He looked up at Richard, his eyes brimming.

"She chose a night when I wouldn't be home until very late. You know how much I worked in those days. She waited until you were asleep and then she took a large number of pills she apparently had been hoarding and drank a significant amount of alcohol. She was determined to end her life. Very determined. By the time I got home, it was too late." His father hung his head, staring at the open napkin in his lap.

"Dad?" Richard reached across the bed and rubbed his father's forearm, bony under the wool sweater. His dad clasped Richard's hand, then moved it away. Richard realized he'd been rubbing hard, not gently as he intended.

"It hurts," his father said, but Richard couldn't tell if he was talking about his dead wife or his arm.

CHAPTER TWENTY-THREE

THE PARTY WAS PREMATURE. CLARE HAD FORCED IT, AS IN DECEMBER SHE FORCED narcissus to bloom indoors. Though the weather cooperated—balmy and in the mid-70s, amazing for February, even in LA—it was a false spring. The pretext for the party was to display their new landscape which, though unfinished, held the promise of beauty. The real reason, she and Richard knew, was to celebrate his return to a normal life; but, like the false spring, the celebration was premature. She invited her mother and their local friends. Audrey and Chuck drove up from San Diego, and Clare's mother managed to restrain both criticism and unsolicited advice for the afternoon. In fact, after she'd had a few gin-and-tonics, Audrey could be, as Marty observed, "a hoot," and to Clare's mystification everyone loved her. Jannie brought her husband, Mike, who was rather shy and serious—the quiet, ill-at-ease husband who marries a vivacious woman to hold up the social end of things. Sara, Marty and Steve arrived as a threesome but Steve broke away quickly and joined Matt at the barbecue. Bob, Richard's friend from the Center, brought his wife, Linda, who turned out to have a friend in common with Sara. Phil Wentworth showed up briefly, offering limp handshakes all around and apologizing for Maria's absence. She had the flu, he explained, and he would need to leave early in order to "be there for her." Sara, still angry at Phil for his wanting to fire Richard, studied her wine glass as Wentworth said his goodbyes.

"Look, it's just the way he is," Clare heard Marty tell Sara.

"I don't have to like him," she responded.

Richard tended bar for a while, alternately drinking club soda and white wine, then circulated among their friends. Clare enjoyed watching him—the confidential way he would lean in as he talked or sling a comradely arm across the shoulders of a friend. It wasn't until she saw Bob watching Richard, taking in his every gesture, that she realized Richard was a little off today: his laugh too loud, his face haggard. She turned away, telling herself that she was reading too much into it, that she had become too watchful and anxious since his diagnosis. She felt someone move to her side—Steve.

"You okay?" he asked.

"Mmmhmm." She wondered what he meant: "okay" how? They weren't as easy with each other now. Ever since what she thought of as their folly in the bedroom, it had been awkward to work together but they managed. And now, at her party to show off the landscape, Steve was trying to make her feel comfortable, and she appreciated it. They walked to the edge of the patio, away from the party's crowd. "This'll look a whole lot better in another month or two," he said. Clare had to agree. So much of the vegetation was newly planted, it hadn't rooted sufficiently and looked inadequate. "There's been a little damage from people stepping off the patio into the beds."

"Who did that?" Clare asked. "The kids?"

Steve looked down into his glass. "Your mother," he answered, a smile playing at the corners of his mouth. Clare could imagine Audrey, cocktail in hand, losing her balance just enough to squash a few of the *Lavandula augustifolias*.

"Great. Just great."

"Where's Matt?" Steve asked. "He was here, barbecuing, but I haven't seen him for the past half hour."

"I saw him going out the gate with Adam," Clare answered, beginning to feel anxious now about Matt as well as Richard. Matt had been behaving himself since he'd started working with Marty, but she still wasn't sure he was reliable.

As if he were reading her thoughts—this was what unnerved her about

Steve—he said, "I'm sure he's not up to any funny business. He'll be back any time." The gate slammed, and they both looked up to see Adam running toward them.

"Mom!" he gasped. Matt followed a little behind his brother, cradling a bundle in his arms. As Matt got nearer she could see he had something wrapped in his sweatshirt, then caught the glint of collar and heard the tinkling tags. Adam pushed his hot face into her chest; whatever he was saying was muffled.

"What happened?" she asked Matt, holding Adam.

Matt looked down, then back at his mother.

"Merlin," he said. "The coyotes got Merlin."

"They killed him?"

Adam tilted his head back and wailed loudly, his eyes squeezed shut. Matt dipped his head, and when he looked up he was crying, too.

"He's not dead, but he's in bad shape, Mom. Real bad. We've got to get him to the vet."

In a moment, Richard was at her side. "I'll deal with the party," he told her. "You take care of your kitty. Sara says she's coming with you."

While Sara drove, Clare called the veterinarian's emergency number on her cell. In the back seat, Matt and Adam laid Merlin on a pillow between them.

"I was walking along the top of the wall with Adam," Matt explained. "We were worried because we hadn't seen him for a while. Then I saw this mess of fur. I couldn't tell it was Merlin, he was lying so still, not even moaning. But then I saw his collar. There was fur scattered around everywhere. I think the coyote must have heard us and run off before he could kill him."

The emergency number connected Clare to a veterinarian on call who directed them to a pet hospital in the San Fernando Valley. He would meet them there, he said.

"Hurry," Adam urged, leaning over the seat.

"Oh, Merlin," Clare cried, reaching back and touching the top of his head with one finger. His eyes were squeezed shut. He appeared to be holding himself perfectly still to contain the pain. "You are the sweetest cat." She thought of him wandering through the coyote-infested scrub on the other side of the wall, then coming face to face with his predator, with no one to help him.

PART THREE

CHAPTER TWENTY-FOUR

"I'm going to lunch? With my boyfriend?" Diana, standing at his office door, either told or asked Richard—it wasn't clear which.

He raised a hand in benediction. "Sure, sure. Have a good time."

Ten minutes later, when he was immersed in yet one more document, Richard's phone rang. Rather than let the call go to voice mail, he picked up.

"Stone?"

Barone again. Richard chose not to respond.

"Stop fucking with me, Stone," the voice said. "You hear?"

"Who is this?"

"You know who this is and you know what I'm talking about."

"No."

"Yes, you do. Keep this up, you'll be … "

Richard didn't hear the rest. He replaced the phone in its cradle and returned to his reading. All he needed to do was get through the afternoon, and then he'd have the weekend to recuperate. TGIF.

~⌒

Sunday. His day of rest. His only day of rest. If there were such a thing in this life he could call "rest." He felt as if millions of tiny electrical currents ran across every square inch of his skin. The pain and irritation were intolerable. The noise wouldn't stop: the clatter of dishes as Clare washed up in the kitchen, the thud of Matt's gigantic shoes on the stairs, the pitch of Adam's voice. And that was just the first assault. Later, there would be the thrum of the shower water, then the whine of lawn mowers, the scream of leaf blowers. Not to mention the traffic noise on the freeway just down the hill: the ambient hum of thousands of cars and trucks hurtling east or west. The neighbor's dogs barked randomly. "Shut up!" Richard screamed from his study's balcony, succeeding only in driving them into a prolonged frenzy of barks and howls. The pool heater started up with a groan, followed by the slurping of its floating sweeper. He gritted his teeth.

"Richard?" Clare appeared on the patio below. She held a dish towel in her hands and squinted up at him. "Are you all right? I thought I heard you yelling at someone."

"You're imagining things."

Clare frowned and went back inside.

Christ, it was like having secret service escorts—all the people who wouldn't leave him alone: Clare, first and foremost; Diana-of-the-grating-voice; and Barone with his threatening phone calls. The guy didn't have the balls to make good on his threats, of course. He was a typical bully: only a threat to the small and the weak, like Maya.

"Richard?" Clare was standing at his study's door. "I'm going to take a walk with Sara. I'll be back in a couple of hours."

He nodded. "Sure. Tell her 'hi' for me." Clare lingered in the doorway, watching him. "What?" he asked. She was really getting on his nerves.

"You're sure you're okay?"

He turned away from her and in a few minutes heard the creak of her steps on the stairs.

~∽

Richard popped the tab off a can of beer and settled into one of the lounge chairs in the garden. He hadn't taken much interest in it, hadn't looked at it carefully, even though when it was being planted Clare had brought the plans to the Center for him to see and had described in great detail what bush would go here, what tree there and why. Steve probably enjoyed talking about that stuff. He put the beer down and walked around the yard. It was greatly transformed. Weird plants—Clare said they were mostly native to the area or else required little watering—tossed restlessly where dried grass and sickly bushes had once languished. He rose and inspected a grouping of peculiar, stumpy palms the landscaper had planted against the wall. Next to them were some twisted bushes that Clare had made a fuss over—"sculptural forms." What bullshit. They gave him the creeps. Gardenias bloomed in a protected area near his favorite lounge chair. Undoubtedly Clare put them there thinking he would enjoy their fragrance. She couldn't have known that he hated gardenias, the scent of his mother's funeral. The cement expanse around the pool had been covered over with dark tiles and studded with Mexican clay planters that he discovered, when he kicked one, were not clay at all but an odd, foam-like substance, made to look like the real thing. Clare had filled them with enormous hibiscus bushes, each six-inch scarlet flower round as a saucer with a single, curved stamen licking out of its center. They looked like something that should be floating in a large, tropical drink. A rum drink, like they used to have on the vacations they took before he went nuts. He could sure use a real drink right now. Maybe he would make himself one, which would mean he ought to back off the Lithium, since he wasn't supposed to drink much when he was taking it. Selva had told him to stick with the medicine, to ride this thing out. But Selva wasn't bipolar. Selva could only imagine what agony he was in.

That night, Richard lay under the sheet, flexing his feet. Clare breathed regularly beside him. How he envied her that ability to sleep through the night. He hadn't slept for days, it seemed. The manic pressure was building. He promised her he'd keep it together but he couldn't. He was losing it. His whole body vibrated, as if a current ran through him. He spent the hours shifting from his right side to his left, trying to ignore the hissing hibiscus, the whispering birch. Merely existing had become so painful that the daily effort it took to live no longer seemed worth it. Legal work was impossible; he had lost the insight, the energy, the talent that was his. Where once he had been able to enjoy the pleasures of life, now getting through the day was a nearly insurmountable task. He was worn down by the strain of pretending that he was normal. It wasn't fair to his family or his friends to force them to endure his presence. His mother's suicide made more and more sense to him.

Clare was awakened at 5:00 a.m. by the sound of rustling in their closet. Richard's side of the bed was empty. She lifted Merlin down from their high bed—it was still too painful for him to jump—so he could find his way downstairs to the litter box. Then, slipping into her robe and padding across the bedroom, she found Richard fully dressed for work, handsome in his dark pinstripe. Navy had always suited him.

"Aren't you full of energy!" She tried for a cheerful, conversational tone, though it frightened her that he wasn't asleep at this hour. He hadn't mentioned any legal case that was particularly pressing. He said he was taking his medications.

"Gotta get outta here," Richard replied, rubbing his hands together. When he noticed her expression, which was worried despite her efforts at concealment, he made a small joke to cover the pressure he could feel building. "Places to go, people to see." He knew it wasn't the slightest bit funny. He knew he had promised her he would guard against another mania, but he could feel his control sliding out from under his feet like a receding wave, causing him to lose his footing and stumble. He was powerless to right himself.

Clare carried Merlin outside and watched him prowl among the bushes, hunting. It had rained last night, buckets of water pounding on the windows. A rain of frogs, Richard always called that sort of downpour. It was something his mother used to say; Clare didn't know why. The landscape she and Steve had designed so carefully was soggy and flattened by the storm. The "sculptural" plants were still upright—stiff, prickly phalluses that would never bend—but the softer plants Clare loved hadn't fared as well.

The garden landscape was a mistake. She had been carried away by the excitement of working with Steve, a sucker for his compliments about her sense of color and all the rest. "Stylish," he had called their garden, and stylish it was—in an LA sort of way. It was sophisticated, savvy—a version of how she once wished herself to be but never was. She was a cottage garden sort of person, a native-plants-with-a-splash-of-annuals gardener, and what she and Steve had created was a landscape exhibit for the Museum of Modern Art.

The landscape was a reflection of Steve's and her joint effort—the push and pull of their infatuation. She missed Steve. She missed the quickening of her pulse when she heard the gate click in the morning and knew he would be there all day. She missed the smell of his skin and the sight of his rough brown hands. She missed the flirtation. Steve had brought romance into her life, brought her a sense of hope when she was bereft. But that was all. Their relationship was all top dressing and no roots. A folly. But she couldn't help missing him. Still, she knew she had done the right thing, choosing her marriage over a silly crush. Richard needed her as much or more as she had once needed him.

It bothered her that Richard was so agitated this morning. She wanted to know how his weekly sessions with Dr. Selva were going, if they were helping quell his anxieties, but Richard got angry whenever she broached the subject. She wished there was something she could do to help him. Maybe she could drop by his office unexpectedly, telling him she had been shopping in the Valley, and go out to lunch with him. Her presence would lend him support without being obvious.

CHAPTER TWENTY-FIVE

Maya Eastman was crying when Richard picked up the phone.

"It's Barry. He's following me again."

"You've seen him following you?"

"No, but I can feel his presence. I have a sixth sense about him. And my astrologist says I'm right."

Richard closed his eyes and rubbed his forehead.

"Look, Maya, he doesn't have any reason to go after you now. You heard what his attorney said—Barry's happy with the settlement, he acknowledges that it's generous and he's ready to get on with his life."

"He lies," Maya snuffled. "He says what he thinks you want to hear." She began to sob.

He took a deep breath. He didn't need this. Just getting through the day was hard enough, the way he'd been feeling, but Maya was clearly distressed; he was her attorney and he needed to take care of her. Besides, she was a good kid. She'd protected him when he was at his most desperate; she never told a soul about the night they'd spent together.

"Where are you?" he asked, his knee bouncing.

"At the studio."

"And your bodyguard?"

"He's here, but I'm still scared."

"Okay. There's a good restaurant not far from my office. It's called Piacere. I'll meet you there at noon."

~

Clare was surprised to find Richard's office empty when she arrived at 12:15. "I thought Richard usually worked through his lunch hour."

Diana raised her eyebrows. "He usually does." She rose from behind her desk and pulled her purse from a drawer, then put on a sweater. "But today he said he was meeting someone for lunch or had a lunch meeting or something like that." Diana shrugged, unperturbed. "I wasn't listening very carefully. But he just left a few minutes ago."

"Did he say where he was going?"

Diana shook her head.

"Maybe he's having lunch with Marty. Will you check?"

Diana's mouth twisted and she huffed down the hall to Marty's office.

"He's not here," she told Clare, "so maybe they're together." Diana hitched her bag over shoulder and opened the door.

"Where would they go, do you think?" Clare asked, following her.

Diana was rushing for the bank of elevators now.

"Try Piacere," she called out as the elevator doors glided shut.

Piacere's lot was full, so Clare had to park on the street and didn't see the black van with a man in the driver's seat parked one row away from the restaurant's side door. The hostess nodded as Clare explained that she was looking for her husband and his partner, who were having lunch here today, then tilted her head in the direction of the dining room. "If they're not in there, they'll be in the bar." Then she turned to the next set of waiting customers.

Clare scanned the nearly full dining room but could find neither Richard nor Marty. The bar on the other side of the restaurant's entrance was dimly lit; she stood at the door, waiting for her eyes to adjust, until she saw in one of the booths a flash of white-blonde hair: Maya Eastman, the soap opera queen, reaching across the table to take the hand of a man whose broad, familiar shoulders were clothed in a navy blue pinstripe jacket. Richard's gold wedding band glinted in the light of the table's candle.

She turned and hurried from the restaurant, waving off the hostess's concern that she hadn't found her husband and his partner. In the safety of her van, she pulled out her cell phone and called Selva. Her hand was shaking and she felt as if she couldn't catch her breath.

"I'm afraid," Clare blurted. "Richard's been agitated, he can't sleep. I was worried about him, so I went by his office. He wasn't there but I found him at a restaurant. He's out to lunch with that woman, that actress—Maya. Do you think he's manic again? You know—hypersexual?" She realized she was gasping.

"Clare, slow down," Selva replied. "Tell me when this started and what you've observed."

He hasn't been himself ever since he got back from Connecticut."

"When did he go to Connecticut?"

"He didn't tell you?"

"I haven't seen him since early December."

Clare was stunned. "But he told me he's been seeing you once a week." Selva ignored that. "Why did he go to Connecticut?"

"He said you told him to go see his father."

"No. I asked him if he had ever asked his father about his mother's death. I never recommend air travel to someone in Richard's state. The time zone changes could tip him over the edge, into a mania."

"But he's not euphoric," she added, hoping this was a good sign.

It wasn't a good sign. He was concerned, Selva said, that Richard might be experiencing a 'mixed state.' "It combines the irritability and agitation of mania with the despair of depression," he told her. "Some people can't bear to live with the loss they now fully comprehend. How soon can you get him in here?"

Clare waited for Richard at his office, but he didn't return. "When will Marty get back?" she asked Diana, who didn't try to hide her irritation as she checked the calendar Sylvia kept for her boss.

"It says here that he has meetings all afternoon; he won't be back."

At three o'clock, Clare gave up her vigil and headed back to Agave to be with the Adam and Matt. Richard's car wasn't in the driveway and he wasn't answering his car phone. The old, familiar dread coagulated in Clare's stomach. By 7:00 p.m. she couldn't stand to wait any longer.

"I'm going to meet Dad," she told the boys. "If he calls looking for me, tell him I'm on my way." Adam nodded. "And ask him where he is."

"But won't he be where you're meeting him?"

"Just ask him."

CHAPTER TWENTY-SIX

RICHARD'S LEXUS WAS PARKED AT AN ANGLE IN THE DRIVEWAY OF THE LA Conchita house, the police tape ripped in two and dangling where the car burst through it. That he hadn't made any attempt to hide his presence seemed to Clare a sign that he didn't care if or when he was found, and that frightened her. The summer fog that usually wrapped the coast in its cold arms this time of evening was hanging back; the air was unusually warm and still, the sun low over the Pacific. A few lights winked from porches in the next block, but at Sara's cabin and the condemned houses around it, all was dark and quiet.

Clare picked her way along the path to the door. She shoved aside the dread that threatened to overtake her and pushed it open. As her eyes adjusted to the dusky room, she made out Richard's form slumped forward on the couch, head hanging, elbows on his knees. A half-gallon bottle of vodka and full glass of clear liquid stood on the low table before him. She took a step closer and saw that there was another object, dark and dull, lying on the table: a handgun.

Richard looked up, then turned his head away.

"Why did you come?" His voice was flat, his breathing ragged.

She moved across the room, turned on the floor lamp next to the couch and knelt by his side. The floor was gritty beneath her knees, embedded with grains of sand that pricked her skin. This was her chance to pull him back from the precipice. Clare wished she had thought about what to say beforehand, not now, when there was no time and the rushing sound in her ears was drowning out all thought.

She stroked the back of his head. "I came for you." She knew at once that she'd made a mistake.

"Then go home."

"I came for all of us—you, me, our boys, your father."

"Don't make me feel worse than I already do."

She gripped his knee to comfort him and to steady her hand's trembling. "Don't you understand how important you are to us?"

Richard shook his head. "It doesn't help."

"I saw you with Maya Eastman today. I saw you having lunch with her, holding her hand." She started to cry. "If I can bear the pain of seeing that and still love you, can't you bear the pain of living? Is everything so terrible that we can't somehow get through this mess together?"

Another mistake. There was no need to bring Maya into it, no need to insert her own pain into the situation. Letting go of him, she sat back on her heels and waited for Richard to remind her how self-centered she was.

Instead, Richard raised his head and leaned towards her. He was deathly pale and sweaty, his skin slick with a gray sheen.

"Maya's dead, Clare." He covered his face with his hands.

It was like a punch in the gut. "How could she be dead?" It made no sense.

Richard threw his head back and wailed, a lament so primal that the hair on the back of Clare's neck bristled. It was excruciating to hear; she wanted to flee and knew she needed to stay.

"I thought she was safe because I negotiated a good settlement," Richard cried. "From the divorce, I mean. But I was wrong. Barry Barone shot her. She told me at lunch that he was going to kill her, and I told her to go home, that she'd be fine. Marty called to tell me a few hours ago. The bastard was lying in wait for her—at her house. When she got home, he shot her. I didn't take her seriously and she died because of it."

"Did they arrest him?"

When Richard looked up, his face was that of a much older man: lined, tired, defeated.

"What difference does it make?"

He reached for the glass of vodka.

"I think I'll have some of that myself," Clare said, heading towards the kitchen. She returned with two glasses.

"I brought you a clean one."

Richard shook his head and a small smile lightened his eyes.

"Clare." He took her hand and pulled her onto the couch beside him. "I'm so sorry. I wish life had turned out differently for us. We got off to a great start, and then it all went downhill."

She started to protest, but Richard placed his finger across her lips.

"Please, I need to explain. I want you to understand why I have to do this." He took a deep breath and continued.

"Nothing's been right ever since I got sick. It's not like I can be cured, so I tried to make the best of things. I've been able to work most of the time. I'm not as sharp as I was before I started taking the meds, and that's hard, but I've been doing a pretty good job. Until today. When I heard about Maya, I thought about how everything I touch turns to shit. I don't want to keep on like this. I feel like I'm already dead. It'll be better for everybody if I check out."

He put his hand on her head in a kind of benediction. "Truly, Kittycat, it's for the best."

Clare rose and paced back and forth across the small, dim space. "Will you listen to yourself? You can't even use the word 'suicide.' You say, 'it's for the best.' Who's it best for? Not for your family."

"Maybe it's best for me."

"Maybe it is. But can't you think about our sons and me?"

Richard leaned against the back of the couch. "I am thinking about our family," he said, and his chin trembled.

"No, you're not." She touched his cheek, but the gesture only served to make his tears come faster.

"I am," he cried. "Really, I am. The boys need a real father, like I used to be. And you—you deserve a good husband, someone you wouldn't have to take care of all the time."

Clare looked down at Richard and wondered how it was that one person came to love another as much as she loved him.

"But I don't want a different husband. I want you."

Clare believed for a moment that she had gotten through to Richard, but then he wrapped his arms across his stomach and began rocking back and forth against the cushions, repeating, "Oh God, oh God." He looked up at her, pleading, "Clare, let me go. I want to die."

She eased him onto his back on the couch, moved a cushion under his head and lay down on top of him, blanketing him with her body, using the pressure of her weight to still his shaking. She had no idea what to do except cover him, to warm him and keep him still. To her relief, his sobbing slowed and his breathing evened out. She closed her eyes and listened to his heartbeat as he slept.

Clare didn't hear the door open, only the intruder's soft chuckle.

"Well, would you look at that!"

She knew immediately who the man must be. Barry Barone was a dark silhouette in the doorway, only the white of his smile visible, reminding Clare briefly, frivolously, of Steve's bleached teeth. She moved her body off Richard's cautiously, hoping that Barone wouldn't notice the gun on the table. Richard was lost in a deep sleep from exhaustion and alcohol, and he didn't stir.

"I want more light," Barone said. "I want him to see what's coming."

"The switch is on the wall behind you," Clare said. She watched Barone grope for the wall with one hand, the gun still trained in her direction, in the other; but he couldn't find the switch, and when he turned to locate it she slipped the pistol into her jacket pocket. She had never held a gun before, much less used one, and she was surprised at its heft. She hoped that Barone wouldn't notice how her pocket bulged and sagged because of it.

Richard roused as light flooded the room and he lifted his head, blinking at Barone in confusion. "Barry?" he asked, sitting up beside Clare.

"That's right," Barone said in a soothing voice. "You got it."

Richard frowned. "What're you doing here?" He was drunk and had a difficult time sitting up.

Barone snorted. "I followed you. I've been following you for months. I know all about you and Maya."

"Maya!" Richard said.

Clare put her hand on Richard's back, silently urging him not to say or do anything to incite Barone further. She glanced up at Barry and saw that he was eyeing the vodka bottle with interest.

"Would you care for a drink?" she asked.

Barone looked surprised, then made a show of thinking it over, first frowning, then breaking into a wide grin.

"Sure. I've got nothing to lose."

Clare felt Richard tense and she gave his arm a warning squeeze. As she reached for the vodka bottle, Barone held out his arm, palm flat.

"Stay right there. I'll take care of this." He filled the glass nearly to the brim while Clare wondered what effect such a large amount of alcohol would have. Would it relax Barone or stoke his anger? It was a chance she had to take.

Barone returned to his place by the door and leaned back against the wall, glass in one hand, gun in the other. He tipped his head back and half the vodka disappeared. He had several days' growth of beard and even at a distance, Clare could smell the funk of his black nylon track suit, which, from its stench, hadn't been near a washing machine in a long time.

The black track suit. The unshaved face. "You know," Clare said. "I think we've met before."

"Yeah?" Barone looked slightly interested. "How so?"

"I think you banged into me with a door once."

Barone's face darkened and she wondered why she had said anything so foolish to him.

"It was an accident, of course."

"Where was that?"

She couldn't tell him it was at Richard's office building; that would surely inflame him. "At a mall in the Valley."

"Huh." Barone shrugged, then looked around as if he just remembered why he was there. He knocked back the second half of his drink and set the glass on the floor.

"Well," he said, "this has been a nice break in a really, really tough day, but it's time to get down to business." He tilted his chin towards Richard.

"Get up, asshole"— he gestured towards the far side of the room with his pistol — "and stand over there."

Clare heard a click and knew from all the detective stories she'd read that it was the sound of the gun's safety being released. Barone pushed himself away from the wall with one hand and pointed the gun at Clare.

"You stay right where you are."

She felt the weight of Richard's gun against her hip, wondered if it had a safety like Barone's or if all she had to do was squeeze the trigger. And if she could manage to put her hand in her pocket without Barone's noticing, could she shoot him through the fabric of her jacket or did she have to take the gun out of her pocket to shoot him? She wished she had watched more television; surely she would know the answers if she had. If there was a safety on the gun she didn't have time to figure out how to release it, and both she and Richard would die.

On the other side of the room, Richard's eyes were on her, not Barone.

"You remember what I said a while ago?"

"Shut up!" Barone screamed, wheeling in Richard's direction.

"Yes," she answered as Barone turned back toward her, waving the gun.

"Both of you—shut the fuck up!"

"I didn't mean it," Richard said to Clare. "I've changed my mind."

Barone spun toward Richard, slipping on the sandy floor and off balance as he pulled the trigger. The sound of the gun was louder than Clare, in all her mystery-reading, ever imagined. Richard's arms flew up and he looked at Clare, astonished, as he fell. As Barone started to crawl across the floor to where Richard lay, Clare pulled the handgun from her pocket and, holding her shaking right hand steady with her left, pulled the trigger—once, twice, she wasn't sure how many times—enough to ensure that Barry Barone would not shoot again that day.

Every life has its clarifying moments when past and future pivot and all is changed. For Richard Stone, no longer young, life turned in the shadow of Rincon Mountain on a dark, ruined street in La Conchita, California. Less than an hour before, he had yearned for death and the everlasting silence it would bring. Now, he found happiness amid sirens, squeaking gurneys and the steady thwack, thwack, thwack of helicopter rotors.

"Look, Lifestar!" Clare said, raising her face to the dark sky. She bent over Richard's gurney and smoothed his hair.

"Lifestar," he repeated. He didn't know she was talking about a hospital's helicopter, and at that moment Richard Stone thought "Lifestar" was the most beautiful word he had ever heard.

EPILOGUE

Perhaps what matters is not human pain or joy at all,
but rather the play of shadow and light on a live body,
the harmony of trifles assembled on this particular day, at this
particular moment, in a unique and inimitable way.

V. NABOKOV, "THE FIGHT"

August 8, 2005

CLARE STOOD WATCH AT THE FRONT WINDOW OF NATHANIEL'S HOUSE—NOW theirs—in Sainsbury, waiting for Richard to return from the airport. Richard's father had lived long enough to see Matt go off to college and Adam start high school and during that time—the happiest in his life, Nathaniel Stone said—he and Clare had become close friends. She was grateful that, if for only a few years, she had the father she always wanted.

It was Nathaniel who helped Clare settle in that first year in Connecticut. Though grateful to be rid of Los Angeles, a place she blamed—irrationally, she knew—for igniting Richard's manic depression, she felt at a loss in Sainsbury and uneasy about Richard's illness. She waited with dread for his next episode: without a steady income, their budget couldn't withstand even one manic spending spree. She imagined that a chance meeting with a neighbor at Fitzpatrick's Market would reveal that Richard had been buying drinks for the house at the local tavern or, picking up their mail at the West Sainsbury Post Office, she'd be surprised at boxes of expensive items Richard had ordered on-line. Though he must have sensed her uneasiness, Nathaniel said nothing. The Yankee inclination to put the best face on everything came as a surprise and an annoyance to Clare, until she began to understand that Nathaniel was teaching her by example how to cope.

"Do you think we could go for a drive today?" he asked. "I haven't gotten my fill of the Fall colors." In that way, he would coax her out of the house, and she found that these excursions lifted her spirits. One day, they stopped at the Catnip Mouse Tearoom in Riverton, one of his favorite spots. It took a while to negotiate the restaurant's uneven walk. Clare held Nathaniel's elbow, hoping to catch him if he stumbled. He didn't like to be fussed over and so drew her arm through the crook of his, acting as if he were taking her on a pleasant stroll. "The Mouse" was a cozy little place decorated in a riotous mix of floral prints that Clare would have shuddered at elsewhere but thought worked perfectly here. Their meal was a leisurely affair, Nat flirting with the waitress, then asking after her children. While they were waiting for the check, Nathaniel slid an envelope across the table to Clare. Inside, she found a savings book from Sainsbury Bank with a balance that stunned her.

"What's this?" she asked.

"For the boys' schooling," Nat said. "I want my grandsons to be able to go to any university and graduate school they please."

"But only my name's on the account."

"Yes. I think we both know why."

"Won't Richard wonder how we're paying it?" she asked.

"I told him I've provided for the boys' educations."

"But Dad ..." she began to protest.

Nathaniel Stone held his hand up. "Richard understands his limitations." He stared across the table at her, unblinking. "Not another word. Ever."

She watched Richard's behavior for signs, uncertain of their portent: was his happiness due to the arrival of spring or was he joyful because he skipped his medication to flirt with mania? Was he sleeping ten hours a day because he was tired from chopping wood or was this the beginning of another downward slide? And if it was, would the coming depression be mild or deadly?

As Clare watched Richard, Nathaniel watched her. One afternoon in late February Richard seemed particularly agitated and had gone for a walk alone. Clare found it difficult to get through the hours of his absence, though she thought she was hiding her concern.

"He'll be back soon," Nathaniel assured her from the depths of his wingback chair.

She nodded, hoping he was right.

"Are you prepared to stay in this marriage?" His question was startling, the kind of thing Sara would ask, but unexpected coming from an old man, and her father-in-law at that.

"I don't know," Clare told him.

"So there's hope, then, if you aren't sure."

"It's difficult," Clare said. "I want so much to be able to trust him."

"Elsa," Nathaniel said, "was very dear to me. I never loved another person that way. But it was a different life than I imagined. After her mental illness began to manifest itself, I had to invent new ways to be close to her. The conventions of normal marriages didn't fit."

"What did you do?"

"It wasn't so much what I did as how I thought. How I changed my definition of what life could be." When he saw that she was waiting, he added, "For one thing, I gave up on the notion of trust. She had limitations, and I learned to accept them. I only wish that Elsa could have."

~⌯

By the time they settled in to Nathaniel's house that first year, Elsa Stone's perennial garden was at rest for the winter. Only the gravel paths that marked its boundary were visible, but they enclosed a tangle of blackberry canes laced with woodbine and clusters of the blackened stumps of last summer's flowers. Most of the original plants had died off or been choked out, but the hardiest ones came back each year.

"This plot was Elsa's life's work," Nathaniel told Clare the first spring. "I have pictures—some in color. I'll find them for you. This flower bed gave her great pleasure." And so began their joint project to recreate Elsa Stone's garden.

At first Clare battled with the dense thicket that once was Richard's mother's carefully designed landscape. When weather permitted, Nathaniel would put on a jacket and sit in a canvas chair just outside the perimeter, reading or chatting companionably. She found the old man's presence soothing.

"Always wanted a daughter," he volunteered one day. "I'm so glad I have you."

Clare's eyes filled and she couldn't speak.

"It's all that matters—your family and your friends."

"Yes," Clare said, taking off her garden gloves and sitting down beside him. "But there are other things you did that matter—your decisions as a judge. They must have affected thousands of people's lives. And the people you represented in lawsuits—you helped them."

Nat waved her words away with his hand, a gesture, Clare recognized, Richard had inherited. "A hill of beans," he said. "Decisions get overturned, clients forget your name." He burrowed more deeply into the sling of the canvas chair. "Elsa killed herself, and for years I wondered if there wasn't something more I could have done. In the end, I realized I did my best, and she knew that."

Using the old photos as a guide, she spent two more growing seasons unearthing Elsa Stone's masterpiece. As she struggled, Clare began to understand the woman she had never known, intuiting her intent: the views she wanted to capture, the plants she paired for the qualities they brought out in each other. To sustain a vision of beauty through the peaks and troughs of her existence had been Elsa's real achievement. Clare painted her garden in all its moods, year after year, season by season. After a time, she added new perennials to the old, uprooted and regrouped the variations, until she could no longer tell which had been Elsa's work and which was hers, where one woman's artistry ended and the other's began. And every year, because it pleased him, she planted for Richard a stand of Kiss Me Over the Garden Gate.

Returning to his roots hadn't been easy for Richard. During their first year in Connecticut, Clare watched him wandering across the snow-crusted fields north of the house, poking at the frozen ground with a broken branch, and wondered if he was thinking of suicide again.

He had imagined that in Connecticut he would write for law journals, become a gentleman farmer, spend more time with his family. Instead, he felt adrift. Then, in late winter of their second year, a well-known Hartford attorney vanished while traveling to a court appearance. Instead of disappearing for six days as Richard had, the lawyer was gone for six weeks, prompting speculation of foul play. When he tearfully turned himself in to the authorities and was examined by a psychiatrist, the diagnosis was bipolar disorder. Richard had followed the stories closely, and the morning the *Hartford Courant* carried the news of the manic-depressive diagnosis, he looked across the breakfast table at Clare with excitement in his eyes.

"I could be of some use," he said.

"But you are of use," she protested, "to us."

"No, no." He waved her away. "I mean I could use what I know about manic depression. What I've learned." He rocked back on two legs of the wooden chair, causing Clare to frown—he would break that chair one of these days. "I don't know why I didn't think of it before. There's probably dozens, maybe hundreds, of guys—and women," he added, watching Clare's face, "who are bipolar. Just like in LA. I never thought ... I could help them deal with the crises. Like Bob did for me. Like you do."

Richard spent the rest of the morning on the phone, calling old contacts and connections of contacts. He seemed to know half the state, Clare thought. Soon he was counseling manic-depressive professionals, lending a hand when it was needed most. The *Hartford Courant* and the *Sunday New York Times* carried feature articles on him. Richard loved the publicity.

At the window, Clare began to fidget. Richard could easily have made it back from Bradley Airport by now, but maybe the plane was late. Or perhaps Sara insisted on stopping at a farm stand. Sara claimed she hadn't known what a real peach tasted like until she had eaten one grown in Connecticut. And if Sara stopped to buy fruit, Marty would want to pick up some wine. Though they decided not to move to Connecticut, they had been true to their promise that they would visit often. Every summer, they came east to spend a month in Sainsbury and a month in Maine, where Clare and Richard would join them. Sara's and Marty's visits were always joyful reunions, the four of them lingering on the terrace late into the night to savor the sparks of fireflies and the scent of the border flowerbed.

Clare made her way along the gravel path to check the guest cottage one more time. She was anxious for Sara and Marty to see the additions they had made to it, and she hoped that its conveniences and comforts would entice them to stay the whole summer. And why not? Marty was retired, after all, and now that they were married—"What took you so long?" Richard asked—neither he nor Sara had reason to stay in California.

As she entered her garden, Merlin leapt out of his patch of catnip and planted himself in the middle of the walkway ahead of her. She stopped to stroke his head and found a tiny gray-green bit of catnip clinging to his fur.

"You need to lay off that stuff," she warned him.

Merlin strolled beside her, waiting as she plucked spent blossoms and the occasional yellowed leaf, then drew up on his back legs, raising both front paws to swat at a moth. His movements weren't as graceful after the coyote's attack, but he had learned to compensate.

Clare returned to her post at the window and Merlin curled into a nearby chair. At last she saw Richard's car in the distance and was flooded by the familiar, irrational relief she always felt when he returned. As he swung the car into the gravel drive, the sun's last rays filtered through the leaves of the ancient sycamore and streamed across Richard's face, dappling it in light, then shadow, then light again.

About the Author

Alexis Rankin Popik, author of *Kiss Me Over the Garden Gate*, is an award-winning short story writer whose work has appeared in *The Berkshire Review* and *Potpourri Magazine*. She has penned numerous articles about local history that have been published in *Connecticut Explored* and the University of Connecticut School of Law and The Hartford Seminary publications. A former union organizer, Popik traveled the country educating shipyard workers about health and safety and founded a labor-management health plan before turning to writing fiction full-time. She lives with her husband in New England.

CPSIA information can be obtained at www.ICGtesting.com
Printed in the USA
BVOW042142280313

316755BV00002B/10/P